Dottie looked at Shea as he ended the kiss and pulled away from her.

"It was either that or die from lack of oxygen." Shea realized his tie was askew. So was the rest of him.

He didn't fool Dottie. "What are we going to do?"

"Do?"

"That wasn't exactly a 'thank you very much for the evening' good-night kiss."

"Dottie, I think I'd better go."

"Forever? You look like you're about to run away."

"I don't run. There's nothing to talk about. You're a very attractive woman, and I'm a man."

"I noticed. And that's all?"

"And your dress doesn't quite cling to you whenever you exhale." She was making this difficult. He knew it was brutal, but it was better to hurt her now than later. "That's it. That's enough."

His words stung, but she didn't believe he meant them. He was afraid of something. What, she didn't know. But she intended to find out.

Dear Reader,

At Silhouette Romance we're starting the New Year off right! This month we're proud to present *Donavan,* the ninth wonderful book in Diana Palmer's enormously popular LONG, TALL TEXANS series. *The Taming of the Teen* is a delightful sequel to Marie Ferrarella's *Man Trouble*—and Marie promises that Angelo's story is coming soon. Maggi Charles returns with the tantalizing *Keep It Private* and Jody McCrae makes her debut with the charming *Lake of Dreams.* Pepper Adams's *That Old Black Magic* casts a spell of love in the Louisiana bayou—but watch out for Crevi the crocodile!

Of course, no lineup in 1992 would be complete without our special WRITTEN IN THE STARS selection. This month we're featuring the courtly Capricorn man in Joan Smith's *For Richer, for Poorer.*

Throughout the year we'll be publishing stories of love by all of your favorite Silhouette Romance authors—Diana Palmer, Brittany Young, Annette Broadrick, Suzanne Carey and many, many more. The Silhouette Romance authors and editors love to hear from readers, and we'd love to hear from *you!*

Happy New Year... and happy reading!

Valerie Susan Hayward
Senior Editor

MARIE FERRARELLA

The Taming of the Teen

Silhouette Romance

Published by Silhouette Books New York

America's Publisher of Contemporary Romance

To Hilda Godges, with thanks,
for making a silk purse out of a sow's ear

SILHOUETTE BOOKS
300 E. 42nd St., New York, N.Y. 10017

THE TAMING OF THE TEEN

ISBN: 0-373-08839-6

First Silhouette Books printing January 1992

MARIE FERRARELLA

was born in Europe, raised in New York City and now lives in Southern California. She describes herself as the tired mother of two overenergetic children and the contented wife of one wonderful man. She is thrilled to be following her dream of writing full-time.

Chapter One

"Mail come already, Mr. Shea," Athena announced. She handed a pile of letters, ads and bills to the tall, dark-haired man seated at the breakfast table. "The mailman must have some heavy date early today, wanting to finish his work so soon."

Shea Delany raised an eyebrow at his Jamaican housekeeper. "And just how would you know something like that?" The inflection in his voice was teasing.

Athena had been with him from the day he had married Sandra, and though the woman's English hadn't improved an iota in fifteen years, her knowledge of him had. By now she knew him inside out and caught his drift. She shook her head until the gray-streaked black hair loosened from the tight bun she always wore.

"Oh no, not with me, Mr. Shea. I'm not seeing him." She laughed heartily. "Athena's way too old for such foolishness."

"You and me both," he agreed, flipping through the letters. Although, if the question were put to him, Shea would have had to say that he was certain Athena had more than a little life left in her even though she was well past sixty.

"You, Mr. Shea?" A perfect, gleaming grin spread across Athena's broad face. "Ha! You prime catch, you are. You have a way to go before you're too old." Athena laughed to herself as she turned and walked into the kitchen. "Too old. That's a good one. Too stubborn, mebbe," she threw over her shoulder just before the swinging door closed behind her. "But for sure not too old."

"Anything for me, Daddy?" Alessandra had been patient for as long as was humanly possible for a thirteen-year-old.

"As a matter of fact—" he leaned over the table, sliding a large brown envelope, postmarked from England, in his daughter's direction "—there is."

Al squealed her delight, happily forsaking the bran muffin she had been toying with for the last five minutes. "It's from Grandmother." Eagerly, she tore away the envelope, then tossed it aside as a book plopped out on the light gray tablecloth.

Shea tried to keep his smile in place at the mention of his mother-in-law. "Yes, I know. What did she send this time?"

"A book on the museums of London."

"Perfect reading for a dynamic shortstop." She never gave up, he thought. Never gave up trying to change people. First Sandra and then Al. Well, at least now there was an ocean between them. Not like the last time.

Shea studied his daughter as she paged through the book. He noticed something different about her expression. Ordinarily, she'd glance at what Louisa sent and then toss it carelessly aside. Louisa's and Al's interests were poles apart. This time, however, Al seemed to be pouring over the book, almost as if she were looking for something. He wondered what it was that held her attention. There were no animals in a book about the museums of London.

He smiled to himself as he watched her. The thick strawberry blond hair was her mother's, as was the slightly cleft chin. But she was all his, he thought, a warm surge enveloping him.

His and the L.A. Zoo's and every stray animal within the city limits. His child, he thought, was a dyed-in-the-wool animal aficionado. And he wouldn't have her any other way.

Al's face clouded over as she paged slowly through the book. He set down his own mail. "What's the matter?"

Al looked up, chewing on her lower lip. "Dad, if you were a guy, would you like me?"

Where had that come from? Oh-oh. Were these the first signs of growing up? She'd been such a tomboy, he thought that perhaps the inevitable would be put off for a little while longer. "I *am* a guy and I love you."

It didn't seem to satisfy her. "What did you like about Mom?"

"Everything," he answered simply. And he had. Absolutely everything, even her weaknesses, although sometimes he wished . . . There was no sense wishing. What was done was done.

"But I'm nothing like her," Al cried. In her hand was clutched the letter that her grandmother had sent.

A letter from hell. That was probably what had caused his normally self-confident daughter's momentary wavering. "I have eclectic taste. Al, what's this all about?"

"Grandmother always writes about how, when Mom was my age, she was the star in the ballet recitals and could play the classics on the piano and—"

"And you don't."

"No." A world of uncertainty was in the single word.

How did he make her see? "There's nothing wrong in being a shortstop if that's what you want to be."

But it wasn't enough. "Daddy, maybe I should, you know, take lessons or something, on how to be a lady." Al's distress rose in her eyes. "Grandmother's coming to visit us and I don't want her thinking I'm some kind of a freak."

"You're not any kind of a freak," he said a little too fiercely. "Change because *you* want to, not because she does." Shea closed his eyes. There had been the same abject expression of sorrow on Sandra's face. Because Louisa hadn't been pleased with her.

Al took a deep breath. "I want to."

"Okay, then I'll help. When's she supposed to arrive?" In his heart, he had hoped never to have to see her again.

Al held up her letter. "Six weeks. Think we can do it by then?"

"It only took God six days to make the earth. We've got more time." His confident tone brought back a smile to Al's lips. "I'll see about making arrangements." He took the letter from her, taking care not to let Al see how annoyed he was over Louisa's visit. "Now promise me that you'll enjoy the rest of the day the way you'd planned, okay?"

"Okay."

When she looked away, Shea's smile faded as he glanced down at the letters and saw that Louisa had sent him one, too. A subdued powder blue envelope with very precise writing on the front. It bore a European postmark. He felt both anger and cold irrational fear stirring.

After all this time, she had written. To him. To Al she wrote every few months. But not to him. This couldn't be good. It was probably about the visit. His first impulse was to throw the letter away, but he knew that to do so would be a mistake. Dreading what he might find, he opened the envelope and read the short letter inside.

"Damn."

Al momentarily forgot the book in her lap. "Something wrong, Daddy?"

Shea looked at his only daughter, his only child, a perfect miniature of Sandra. Except, he thought, Sandra would have never dressed in blue jeans and a T-shirt with a baseball team emblem splashed across the front of it. Nor would she have worn her hair as boyishly short. Louisa would have never allowed it, even if Sandra had been so inclined.

And now she was trying to change Al. "Nothing, honey, just mumbling to myself."

Al eyed her father suspiciously. "Sounded like you said 'Damn.'"

Shea pretended to look at her sternly. "Al, you know I don't like you to repeat words like that."

"Then don't say them," she said with a pert toss of her head.

Thirteen going on thirty, he thought. He shoved the letter into the pocket of his jacket. "I'll try to remember that, Squirt."

Al grinned. "Are you going to come to the game this afternoon?"

That was more like her, he thought. Shea looked down into her green eyes, alive with mischief and hope. She might resemble Sandra, but she had his eyes. His soul, he thought. He had loved baseball as a kid, but then there hadn't been time to play. The business of living, of making it through another day alive, had been all consuming.

Quickly, he went through his schedule. He could postpone a meeting this afternoon and get away. "Wouldn't miss it for the world."

Al pushed her chair back and grabbed her mitt. "I'm going to go practice now."

He glanced at his watch. He wasn't due in the office until ten. "Wait a few minutes and I can drop you off when I drive to the office."

But Al shook her head. "Steven Palmer's mom is picking me up. I promised to show Steven how to throw a slider." She winked artfully. "He's kind of cute."

A manipulator already, Shea thought with a fond shake of his dark head. She might look like a tomboy, but she was very definitely a young woman in the making. "Guess I'll have to ride to the office alone."

There was a short, staccato blast of a horn. "That's Mrs. Palmer now. The game's at four, Dad." She kissed her father's cheek just before she dashed to the front door. "Be there."

"Who's the kid and who's the parent?" he called after her.

Al dodged to avoid colliding with Athena as the woman appeared with Shea's coffee. "We'll work it out later," Al promised as she yanked open the door. "And thanks, Dad, for understanding."

"That's what I'm here for. Say hello to Mrs. Palmer for me," he said just before the door slammed.

Athena pursed her lips in disapproval. The expression didn't negate the love apparent in her deep brown eyes. "In my country, thirteen-year-olds don't order their fathers around like that." She set the cup in front of Shea and began clearing the table. The woman raised her eyes and noticed Shea's sober mood. "Something troubling you, Mr. Shea?"

Shea closed his fist over the letter in his pocket, and with a tired sigh, he rubbed the bridge of his nose. He'd hoped that all this was behind him when Louisa had left for Europe. Apparently not. "Louisa's arriving in the States in six weeks."

Athena's face grew grave. She had been in Louisa's employ before she took on the job of housekeeper for the Delany family and was well acquainted with Louisa's character. She put Shea's worst fears into words. "Will there be trouble, Mr. Shea?"

I hope to God, not, he thought fiercely. "No, no trouble this time, Athena. I'm just not going to let it happen."

It wasn't much, but for seven hundred dollars a month, it was all hers. Dottie McClellan slowly turned around the small office. *Her office.* It didn't matter that there was barely enough room to hang her newly issued diploma on the wall. It was hers.

A tiny alcove served as a reception area for the secretary Dottie still didn't have and couldn't afford at any rate. The inner office was hardly larger. It was dominated, engulfed really, by a brand-new oak desk and chair, a gift from her brother Shad and his wife, J.T., and the stereotypical sofa, compliments of Angelo Marino, her foster brother.

Cozy, Dottie thought, surveying it now with as critical an eye as she could muster. The office was small, but not claustrophobic, just cozy, which was exactly what she had wanted. No cold, austere room that would make her patients nervous. She was here to help, not judge, not oversee. Later, when the time came to branch out because of a bigger practice, her goals would be no different.

The impressive black phone, with its one live and three yet dormant lines, rang, startling her. It was too soon to expect a potential patient's parent to be calling. Still the tiny, unfounded hope was there. Stranger things had happened. She *was* now on the referral list.

Hope faded with the sound of J.T.'s low, breathy voice. Disappointment lasted exactly ten seconds before Dottie's natural exuberance took over. "Hi, how are things with my favorite sister-in-law, slash, accountant?"

"Busy."

Dottie flipped the empty pages of her brand-new appointment book. "Lucky you."

"I take it that you don't have a full schedule yet."

Dottie laughed. She knew she had a reputation with those she loved as being slightly over-zealous when it came to practically everything. She was always inclined to do two things at once while taking on more.

"Nope." She closed the book and pushed it to the side of her desk. "But then, I've only been a bona fide child psychologist for two weeks, according to the degree that now hangs so beautifully on my soothing pale blue wall." She glanced at it now with no small pride. "My appointment book isn't exactly bulging at the seams."

"What is it, exactly?"

Dottie caught the hopeful inflection on the other end and wondered what J.T. was up to. It wasn't like her sister-in-law to be devious. But then, J.T. had trouble asking for favors straight out. "Empty."

"I remember what that's like. When I was starting out, I had to go begging for accounts."

Dottie leaned back in her chair and rocked. "I plan to hold off for at least one more week before I start stealing patients from other, more prosperous child psychologists." She waited exactly five seconds for J.T. to jump in and tell her why she had called. When she didn't, Dottie asked. "Okay, J.T., what's on your mind? Besides debits, credits, my adorable nephew and my not-so-adorable brother, I mean."

J.T. laughed. "Can't this just be a regular phone call?"

"It can be. But I have a feeling that it isn't. You have that how-do-I-say-this catch in your voice."

J.T. didn't bother hiding her amusement. "You're going to make a terrific psychologist, Dottie."

Cradling the telephone against her shoulder and head, Dottie began arranging pens and pencils. Again. "You might think of passing that along to some of your clients."

"I already have, which is what this phone call is all about. I think I have a client for you."

"In accounting, they're clients, J.T. In my new, yet untried profession, they're called patients."

"Well, this isn't a patient, exactly."

Dottie sat up and dragged her hand through her hair. One long blond hair caught on her ring and she winced as it was yanked out. "J.T. you've been married to my brother too long. You're not making any sense at all." She heard J.T. let out a deep breath.

"Let me start from the beginning."

"Please."

"I have this client, Shea Delany."

Dottie was impressed. "As in Delany Antiques?" She thought of the grand showroom she had passed each day on her way to the UCI campus.

"Exactly. He was one of my very first clients. I've known him for years. Anyway, he came by today to have his books worked on and he seemed rather preoccupied. It took a while, but I finally got him to tell me what was wrong. It seems he has this problem."

Restless, Dottie pulled out a pad and began to doodle. "Certainly not financial, I'm sure," Dottie murmured. She recalled reading about Shea Delany in the business section of the newspaper. He was a self-made man who had worked his way up from nothing and now owned a number of antique stores in California and Arizona. There had been a grainy photograph with the article. She remembered thinking he was cute.

"No," J.T. was saying, "this problem involves his daughter."

Dottie began to draw a series of falling stars. "Ah, the plot thickens."

"She's a tomboy."

Dottie grinned, remembering her leap off the roof of Mama Marino's house, a pink towel tied to her back. If that carob tree hadn't been where it was, she would have probably broken her neck instead of just her leg. Papa Marino had lectured her for weeks, in between hugging her tightly and bringing her ice cream. "Weren't we all? I take it he's not happy about that."

"Actually Shea worships the ground Alessandra walks on, designer athletic shoes and all."

Okay, the man wasn't a male chauvinist. Nice to know. "So, what's the problem?"

"Well, maybe I'd better let him explain."

Dottie shrugged, pushing aside her drawing. "He certainly can't make it any more obscure than you have. Is he there with you?"

"No, as a matter of fact, he just left. But I suggested that he discuss this matter with you. He's having lunch at Mon Petit Chateau at twelve-thirty. I told him that you'd be there if everything was all right with you. Is it, Dottie?"

Why not? It sounded interesting in a confused sort of way, and if she could help, she would. Dottie had chosen her profession because she loved helping. Anyone and anything. She was softhearted by nature. "Right now I'm not doing much of anything except sharpening pencils and doodling. I can be there by twelve-thirty."

"I'd really appreciate it, Dottie. I'd help him out myself, but I'm up to my elbows in work and Shad threatened to take away my calculator if I'm late for dinner one more night."

Dottie laughed. "When he threatens, he certainly goes all out. Don't give it another thought."

"Thanks, you're a gem. Oh, one more thing."

"Shoot."

"He's kind of a private person."

Dottie grinned. "My specialty."

"No, I'm serious."

"So am I. Just leave it to me."

Obviously he didn't photograph well, Dottie thought looking at the man the maître d' had pointed out to her. The picture in the newspaper hadn't begun to do him justice. Shea Delany was sitting alone at a table for two, oblivious to the not-so-covert glances of various women in the small, fashionable restaurant. His face was movie-star perfect with long, aristocratic planes and angles that gave him a rather regal, sensual look. The only problem that he could have, she thought, was keeping women at bay.

Enough sighing on the sidelines, she told herself, her grip tightening slightly on her purse. Walking purposefully around a young couple who were moving much too slowly for her liking, Dottie crossed to Shea's table.

He was even better close up. J.T. had excellent taste in clients and friends, Dottie thought. "Mr. Delany?"

Shea raised his eyes when he heard the soft, low voice say his name. The voice fit the woman, he decided, wondering if this was J.T.'s sister-in-law. J.T. was subdued elegance; this woman reminded him of a blond, mischievous Gypsy. It was the way she stood, relaxed, sure of herself, her eyes smiling. She certainly didn't look like a trained professional. "Yes?"

"I'm J.T.'s sister-in-law, Dottie McClellan." Dottie put out her hand and smiled broadly.

She was warm and friendly—not at all what he'd expected. He had envisioned someone more somber and scholarly, in keeping with the therapist Louisa had sent Sandra to when she had told her mother that she wanted to marry him.

Shea rose and took Dottie's hand. "I'm glad you could make it," he said as he held out a chair for her then seated himself.

Dottie laughed. "It wasn't as if I had to be pried away from my desk." She leaned over in a way Shea found exceedingly intimate and placed her hand on his forearm. "I have to be honest with you in case J.T. neglected to mention the fact. I've only had my degree for a little over two weeks. It's still warm."

As was her breath upon his face, Shea thought, feeling a normal, physical pull. He glanced at her hand and Dottie removed it smoothly. At least one of them was comfortable about this, he thought, still not knowing if this was such a good idea.

The waiter approached, then stood at a discreet distance, waiting. "Would you care for something to drink?" Shea asked Dottie.

She longed for a ginger ale, but thought she'd sound more professional if she asked for something a little more sophisticated. First impressions lasted. "I feel like having something light. A white wine would be nice."

Shea nodded. "Two glasses, please," he told the waiter who then disappeared.

Shea looked down at his hands. This was awkward. A quick mind and a glib tongue had helped him get out of his neighborhood twenty years ago. Then a deepening layer of studied sophistication had brought him to his present position. But he had no precedent for this, nothing to really draw on. "I'm not quite sure I know how to start."

The more awkward a person became, the more Dottie would feel herself softening. Whatever this man needed, she'd find a way to help. That was instantly settled in her mind. She had always been a sucker for sad eyes. Shad had teased her time and again, and this man had them. "The beginning always helps."

"All right." But then he hesitated. Somehow, this was all wrong, Shea thought. Al didn't need to change just because Louisa was coming. "Look," he began hesitantly. The faster this was said, the better. He had inconvenienced her enough. "I don't want a child psychiatrist—"

"Psychologist," Dottie cut in.

His momentum was shattered. "Excuse me?"

She smiled easily. "I'm a psychologist, not a psychiatrist. There is a difference."

He nodded, accepting the correction. Shea tried again. "What I really want is someone to play Henry Higgins—"

"Pygmalion," Dottie interjected, then bit her lip. She hadn't meant to correct him. It had just slipped out.

Shea stopped. "What?" The waiter returned and placed both goblets of wine on tiny rose-colored napkins before retreating again.

Dottie slipped her fingers around the goblet's stem, though she didn't drink. She hoped she hadn't annoyed him. *"My Fair Lady* is really based on Shaw's *Pygmalion."*

Something else he wouldn't have known that Louisa would have probably found important, he thought irritably. "Do you always correct people while they're talking?"

Dottie watched the way he unconsciously crumpled the napkin in his hand. Careful, she counseled herself. He was tense. The tension only served to make him look that much more sensual. Her own expression became the last word in innocence. "Sorry. No offense."

He softened. "None taken." He needed someone with a broad range of knowledge to infuse some culture into Al's mind. He'd do it himself, but he had a feeling that at this point in her life, Al needed a woman she could relate to. A psychologist wasn't what she really needed. She'd probably only wind up analyzing motives. "Besides, there's nothing wrong with Al's—with Alessandra's—mind."

"I never said there was," Dottie said easily, her eyes on his face.

She was interrupting again, but he let it pass. "It's just that she's lacking in certain, shall we say, social graces that my mother-in-law—Al's grandmother—thinks are essential and that Al has suddenly decided she needs."

Dottie studied him. He didn't seem like the type who would care about bending over backward for the sake of someone else's beliefs if they interfered with his own way of thinking. "All this trouble for a mother-in-law?"

Shea was struck by Dottie's straightforward manner. She certainly didn't pull punches, but the question was delivered with such sincere interest that he didn't feel right about backing away from it entirely. "All this trouble for my daughter," he corrected. "Besides, it's a little more involved than that."

"Oh?"

The single word held a whole range of emotion behind it, coaxing him to go on. "You're waiting for me to tell you, aren't you?"

Dottie grinned and dimples formed in both cheeks. "J.T. didn't mention that you were astute."

Flattery was something he always held suspect, even when the person delivering it looked so guileless. "Did she happen to mention that I'm a rather private person?"

Dottie knew evasion when it stared her in the face. She also knew that she usually found a way around it. She lifted her glass, taking a sip. The wine made her feel warm. It made her inclined to be even more open than she was normally. "She might have said something like that."

"But you didn't think that was important enough to pay attention to?" He had gotten to where he was by sizing people up quickly.

He had her number, she thought, and she had his. She grinned over the glass before she took another sip. Wine had certain advantages over ginger ale, she decided. "Nope."

"Well, I'm afraid I am." He tried to be stern, but he was finding her smile increasingly infectious, although at the moment, he felt as if he had nothing to smile about.

There was a time and a place for total privacy, but she didn't think that this was it. "Unless this is a matter of national security, Mr. Delany," she placed her glass on the table, "I think you'd better give me a few more personal details."

The conversation was not quite going in the direction he had anticipated. Shea was used to having his wishes carried out. But challenges had always intrigued him, even if they encroached on his territory. "Why?"

"Well, for one thing, because I work better when I have all the information. It's hard constructing something in the dark." *And because, quite frankly,* she added silently, *I want to know.*

"Is that a sample of your enlightened philosophy?"

There was something in his eyes she couldn't quite read yet. Anger? Fear? Of what and who? "Why are you angry with me?"

He was annoyed with himself for letting his temper get the best of him. It wasn't her fault that Louisa Taylor Babcott disapproved of him, had always disapproved of him, first as a husband, then as a father. He wanted to apologize, but couldn't quite find the words. Apologies were never simple for him. "I'm not angry with you. I'm angry—annoyed," he corrected, "with Louisa."

Dottie suspected that his anger was not a pretty thing once it was let loose. "Poor Louisa."

He laughed shortly. If it was anything the woman was not, it was poor, except perhaps in the area of human kindness. "Just the opposite."

"Oh?"

He drained his glass, then sat contemplating the empty goblet, twisting it around in his fingertips as if he had never seen it before. He wasn't seeing it now. He was thinking of all the gifts she had been sending Al over the years. The European cruise she had offered Sandra if only she wouldn't marry him. "She thinks she can buy anything she wants."

Dottie nodded knowingly. "Like your daughter." Where was the girl's mother, she wondered. Dead? He hadn't mentioned her and Dottie assumed that he would have, if she were a vital part of all this. J.T. had a lot of information to fill her in on, she thought, since Shea was obviously reluctant to do so.

Shea raised his eyes from the glass until they met hers. Her eyes were soft, blue and full of understanding, even though she knew next to nothing about all this, he realized. "Like my daughter," he echoed.

"Louisa's your mother-in-law," Dottie surmised.

"Yes."

"And if Al isn't transformed into a young Audrey Hepburn—" she smiled, falling back on his reference to *My Fair Lady* "—you're afraid that your mother-in-law will find a reason to find fault with you or perhaps even take her away from you." It didn't exactly make any sense to her, but that was the best she could do with the pieces he was handing her.

A grudging smile slid over his aristocratic features. He looked so handsome that a knot formed in Dottie's stomach. She had to remind herself that this was business.

"No, there is no way Louisa could take Al away from me. This is basically Al's wish, although fueled, I suspect, by Louisa. Let's put it this way. I like Al just the way she is. But it wouldn't hurt to infuse a little culture into her—since she wants it that way—to placate Louisa and hopefully send her back across the ocean to her lair." He smiled, realizing how much he had just said. "You're pretty good at ferreting things out."

"So I'm told." She grinned. "Anything else you don't want to tell me?"

He laughed, this time with genuine pleasure. "Why don't we work it out as we go along?"

"Sounds fair enough to me. When do you want me to start?"

"Are you busy tomorrow?"

She smiled and Shea thought there was something terribly disarming in her smile. "I am now."

"Would you care to order?" a voice asked to her left.

Dottie was surprised to see the waiter standing next to her. She had gotten so involved with Shea, she had been oblivious to everything else. "I'd love to," she said, picking up her menu. She grinned at Shea. "Ferreting always makes me hungry."

As Shea picked up his own menu, he couldn't help wondering if he was somehow getting more than he had bargained for.

Chapter Two

Dottie needed answers and she wanted them before her next meeting with Shea. Lunch with him yesterday had been a very pleasant experience, but had yielded precious little information. J.T. was the obvious one to see.

When she arrived at J.T.'s two-story stucco house, no one answered when she rang the doorbell, but she heard raised voices coming from the rear of the house. Dottie followed them into the backyard.

She found Shad and his stepson, Frankie, playing catch. Her sister-in-law was nowhere to be seen.

"Okay, what've you been doing with J.T.?" Dottie asked as she walked onto the patio. Shad threw a fast pitch to Frankie. The boy dived for it.

"Whatever happened to 'hello'?" Raising his arm high, Shad caught the ball Frankie shot back to him.

"Hello." She moved closer to the two, standing clear of Shad's arm. "What've you done with J.T.?" she repeated. "I need to talk to her."

Shad threw another fastball. Frankie stretched and made an excellent running catch. "She said something about needing some time alone, so she went to the mall." The ball smacked into his glove.

"Which is, of course, deserted." Frustrated, Dottie watched as Frankie made another running catch. "Well, if she wanted to go shopping, she could have called me."

"She said you'd be busy." Shad had to strain to catch the ball Frankie threw. "The kid's good," he said with pride. "A few more years and he can support us with a career in the majors."

She laughed. "I'll give you this, when you dream, you dream big."

He grinned at her. "Is there another way?"

"No, I guess not."

"How'd you like that last catch?" the gangly fourteen-year-old called over to them.

"A couple of years from now, they'll be making baseball cards with your picture on them," Dottie told him.

Frankie beamed in response. "I wish!"

"What are you up to today?" Shad asked as he threw the next pitch.

Dottie retreated back to the shade of the covered patio. "That's what I wanted to see your wife about. She referred Shea Delany to me and there are a few things I want to clear up before I go on with this." The next ball Shad threw missed coming near Frankie by a mile. "It's a cinch *you're* not going to be anyone's first draft choice."

He let her teasing observation pass. Instead, he turned and looked at her. "What are you doing with Shea?"

She sighed, thinking of the man in the pearl gray suit. "Nothing, I'm afraid. It's his daughter who's the problem. Something about needing to be infused with culture."

"And J.T. sent him to *you?*"

"Thanks, I needed that." She went up to Shad and gave him a shove with the flat of her hand.

"Hey, no mauling the pitcher," Angelo called out as he walked into the backyard. He was wearing his favorite worn T-shirt and a baseball cap. Chestnut brown hair curled all around the perimeter like a halo. "Only I get to do that." Bending down, he kissed Dottie's cheek. "Hi, kid, what're you doing here?"

"Twiddling my thumbs. My sister-in-law, who is the only one I can ask certain questions of, is shopping away her Saturday and I'm stuck with this inept ball player."

"Inept?" Shad cried indignantly.

"You messed up the last pitch," she pointed out.

"Here, Ange, take over for a minute." Shad tossed his glove at his foster brother and took hold of Dottie's arm.

"What?" She could see by the look in Shad's eyes that he was about to play Big Brother.

"I know I shouldn't be asking this of a woman who takes in every stray within a twelve-mile radius, but are you sure you want to get involved with Shea and his daughter?"

She didn't understand. "Why not?"

"For one thing, I thought you'd want to get started on your career." He picked up a can of soda from the six-pack on the table, popped the top and took a long drink. "A career, I might add—" he met her eyes over the green-and-gold can "—that I helped pay for."

She took the can from him, took a sip, then handed it back to him. "Don't worry, you'll get it back."

Shad put the can on the frosted glass tabletop with a sharp bang. "That's not the point and you know it."

"Yes, I know it." She patted his cheek, then rubbed her hand on the back of her shorts. He was sweaty. "The point is that you like bossing around your little sister."

He rubbed the perspiration from his forehead with the back of his hand. "Don't try any of that psychology stuff on me."

"That's not psychology." She sniffed. "That's experience."

Shad sighed as he watched Angelo pitch to Frankie. "I guess no one could ever tell you what to do."

Dottie turned toward Shad, affection written on her face. "But you keep trying, don't you?"

"I have to." He gave Frankie the high sign as the boy made another difficult catch. "It's my job."

"Thank God you don't rely on that to earn a living, or you'd be forced to be a gigolo and live off J.T.'s money."

As Angelo threw out another ball, Shad looked back at his sister. Five years her senior, he had always felt protective of her, even before they had been on their own. "Seriously, Dottie, do you think it wise to steer off the track at this point?"

There was something else behind what Shad was saying, but she knew him well enough to realize that he'd tell her in his own time. "I'm not on track yet, Shad. It's not as if I had to reshuffle a whole slew of patients to fit this in."

"What'll you do if you *do* get patients while you're busy with Shea's daughter?"

She shrugged. A balancing act was nothing new to her. She had gone to school and held down a full-time job. She enjoyed challenges. "I'll work it out as I go along. Besides, this isn't going to take very long. Shea mentioned something about six weeks. Shad, the man needs my help—and he's willing to pay."

Shad recognized the stubborn look on his sister's face. It meant that her mind was made up. "Well, I guess I can't change the spots on a leopard."

Frankie, sweat curling and darkening his blond hair, joined them on the patio. Angelo tossed aside the glove and crossed over to Dottie's other side. Dottie held out a cold can of soda for each of them as she looked at Shad over her shoulder. "Not even with a laundry marker."

Shad laughed, taking another drink of his soda. "Glad to see a degree hasn't changed your succinct way of stating things."

"Not even *what* with a laundry marker?" Angelo asked. Though they had spent most of their childhood and teen years together and were as close as three people could be, at times there was still a special communion between Shad and Dottie.

"Change my spots," Dottie said.

"What spots?" Frankie looked at her curiously.

"Your dad was referring to my stubborn streak." She turned toward Angelo, offering him a wide smile. "I'm not stubborn, am I Angelo?"

Angelo looked from Shad to Dottie then communed with his can of soda. "How do I answer this and remain undamaged?"

Frankie came to his rescue. "I get the picture."

Dottie looked at all three fondly. "Men."

Shad nudged his stepson. "That's a sign of her razor-sharp mind." He quickly raised an arm to fend off the blow he anticipated. To his surprise, it didn't come.

She saw the question rise in his eyes. "I'm a child psychologist now. I don't hit. Much."

Shad dropped his arm. "I knew there was a reason I sent you to college."

"Well, since J.T. isn't here, I'd better get going."

"When are you seeing Shea?" Shad wanted to know.

"In half an hour." She saw Shad frown and almost asked him why. But if he hadn't been inclined to tell her when they were alone, he certainly wasn't going to say anything now that Frankie and Angelo were with him. She let it go for now. "'Bye. Say hi to J.T. for me," she called out as an afterthought. "And tell her I'll give her a call later tonight."

"I'll warn her," Shad promised.

Al studied the scuff marks on her sneakers. There were a multitude crisscrossing over the once-white rubber. She tugged absently on her pink laces. "You mean she's a shrink?"

Shea didn't like the hurt confusion he heard in his daughter's voice. Damn, he should have just told her that Dottie was a friend. But he had never lied to Al. Never. "No, a psychologist."

Al turned her face up to him. A smattering of freckles dusted her nose and meandered to her cheeks, where they finally faded away. "What's the difference?"

"About four years of school. A psychiatrist goes to medical school." He moved to put his arm around her, but Al slid off the sofa, still clutching the baseball in her hand.

She looked down at the ball, then let it drop on the sofa as if she was suddenly ashamed of it. A myriad of emotions seemed to be colliding within her. "Think she can help me?"

He discovered that he still wasn't a hundred percent in favor of this idea. He liked her just the way she was. "Don't make it sound as if you need reconstruction, Al. But yes," he said in answer to the slightly impatient look that rose into her eyes, "she can help you with what you want to learn. I was told that she's very good with kids." Al's frown deepened. "Young people." Obviously, that wasn't what she wanted to be called either. "What is it you want me to call you?"

She tossed her head. "A young woman."

A smile played on his lips. "That's going to take me some time to get used to, but I'll work on it." He studied her intense expression for a moment. "Al, do you feel that I did something wrong in the way I raised you?"

He didn't need to be reassured. He just wanted to hear her opinion. In his own mind, he had done everything correctly, had always been open, fair and understanding with Al. He had given her, he felt, her own head. He had been determined to raise her with as much love and sense of security as he could possibly give her. Sandra had told him that she had never really felt loved, had always felt hemmed in. And inadequate. She had always tried to please her mother. He had never forced Al into that mold. Just having her be Al pleased him.

He watched Al's face cloud over with concern. "You've always been the best."

Nothing warmed his heart more than Al's instinctive loyalty. This was his wealth, not the accounts that bore his name or the securities his broker purchased for him. This and only this meant anything. If at times he longed for a woman to hold, to share his heart with the way only two lovers could, well, there had been Sandra and the memory of their life together would sustain him. Besides, the risks involved in loving were too costly.

"Okay, I just wanted to get that cleared up. And, are you sure you want to get into all this? It's a far cry from your softball game—in which you played brilliantly, I might add."

She flashed him the wide, bright smile he had always loved. "Thanks. Yeah, I'm sure."

"Yes, I'm sure," he corrected.

"What?" She stared at him, confused.

"If you want to get into this all the way, you're going to have to learn how to speak correctly. It's 'yes,' not 'yeah.'"

"What's the difference?"

"A firm grip on education, Squirt." He tugged at her hair fondly.

Al looked as if she wasn't sure whether to laugh or not. She cocked her head. "Is 'Squirt' cultured?"

"Only as far as you're concerned." He gave her a hug. She was growing up, he told himself and all this was natural and right. Louisa's coming was only a catalyst to set it off. Maybe the woman could accomplish something positive for a change.

But in his heart, he doubted it.

"Huh?" She sank back down on the sofa, looking up at her father's face.

"That's why we need Ms. McClellan, or someone like her."

Her frown deepened. "I don't understand."

"Exactly." He touched her nose again, indicating the correctness of her answer. "And Ms. McClellan is going to help you understand."

"A psychologist can do that?"

"This psychologist can," he told her. "According to my accountant."

"Your accountant?" She jumped up from the sofa again, horrified. "Dad, you're putting my life in the hands of an accountant?"

He tried not to smile at her dramatics. "Why not? I put my affairs into her hands."

"Her?" Al echoed, her thunder evaporating.

"My accountant is a woman. J.T. McClellan."

"Oh." Al rolled the information over slowly in her mind. "Then it's okay."

Shea grinned. "I thought that might meet with your approval."

He supposed that these lessons were for the best after all. Al would certainly benefit and it would erase that small, nagging doubt that lived in the back of his mind, the doubt that Louisa would find a way to lure Al away somehow, legally or with guile. She could make Al want to come live with her, turn her head about the "advantages" she could show her. If Al begged, he wouldn't be able to deny her. He had never denied his daughter anything. He didn't want to think of this as an emotional tug-of-war, but he was going to use whatever methods he had at his disposal to make certain that Louisa didn't somehow cause Al to turn from him.

Louisa had done that with Sandra. She'd been unable to live with the fact that her daughter wanted to be married to him rather than live with her. The end result had been disastrous. There would be no repeat performance, no danger of psychological warfare. Shea was stacking the deck in his favor. If his daughter was about to enter young womanhood and wanted to be introduced to the world of culture, he'd present it to her on a silver platter. If Dottie didn't work out, he'd hire someone else who would.

Al put her arms around his neck and hugged him as hard as she could. "Thanks, Dad."

Shea patted his daughter's hand and knew that he would go to the wall, to any lengths humanly possible, to keep this child in his life. No one could convince him that he hadn't done a good job. She was all he had ever cared about since Sandra had died. It had taken a long time to pull himself out of the tailspin into which Sandra's sudden death had thrown him. But he had done it. Not for himself, not for the money, which meant nothing to him anymore. But for Al. His daughter's happiness was all that mattered to Shea.

The doorbell chimed. Shea and Al exchanged looks. Al's was eager. "Is that her?"

He glanced at his watch. Right on time. "That's her. The lady seems to be very punctual."

"That's good, huh?"

"A lady is always on time." He noticed the sudden thoughtful look on his daughter's face. Was she having second thoughts? "What's on your mind?"

"Why doesn't Grandmother like you?"

He hadn't expected that. But then, Al had always been perceptive. It was a long story, too long to burden her with. Too long and too hurtful. He had never said anything against the woman to Al. That would have been luring Al into the schism that existed between Louisa and him. He gave Al the highlights in a nutshell. "Because I married her daughter," he said, knowing that didn't explain anything.

"Didn't she want Mom to be happy?"

He laughed affectionately. "Not with someone she hadn't chosen for her."

"Grandmother's a snob?"

Shea couldn't help himself this time. He laughed, giving Al a quick hug. "Of the highest water."

That was the way she first saw them together. Hugging. It gave Dottie a very good feeling. She remembered what it had felt like, climbing up on Salvatore Marino's big, roomy lap. He'd hold her, one arm wrapped around her shoulders, a storybook in his other hand. She recalled wonderful hours filled with fairy tales. It was safe and warm there on his lap, and Dottie had felt as if nothing in the world could ever hurt her again.

"The woman, she is here, Mr. Shea," Athena announced. She stood in the room a moment longer, as if to assess the situation, then walked away, nodding her head. Dottie watched her, intrigued. She had absolutely no idea what was going on in the housekeeper's mind. But she couldn't shake the feeling that nothing ever happened in this house without the woman knowing about it.

Yes, Shea thought, the woman was certainly here. She wore her hair in a braid, not loose the way she had at the restaurant. It gave her a more youthful appearance. Too youthful. She was dressed casually, in a two-piece gold dress with wide dolman sleeves that still couldn't hide the fact that nature had been very generous with Dottie McClellan.

Again he felt it. Something insistent buzzed and hummed within him every time he was near her. Maybe it was just a matter of old habits coming back to haunt him. He'd had a wild streak once, enjoying the company of women whenever the opportunity arose, going from one to another without looking back. Looking for love in all the wrong places, he supposed. Until Sandra. He didn't want to think about that, not now.

Shea released his daughter and straightened up. "How long have you been standing there?"

"Long enough to know I made the right choice when I said yes," Dottie answered.

He didn't like being analyzed or having judgments passed on him, even favorable ones. He told himself the situation was making him too touchy. Shea took his daughter's hand in his, forming a silent alliance with her.

The girl was looking Dottie over carefully. It wasn't evident to Dottie from Al's expression whether or not she had passed whatever test Al had in mind. Well, she'd work on that, too. If she wasn't up to challenges, she was in the wrong field.

Dottie put out her hand to the girl. "Hi, I'm Dottie McClellan. And you're Al."

Al looked a little uncomfortable about being addressed by her nickname. "That's what my Dad calls me," she said as she shook Dottie's hand.

Shea looked at his daughter in surprise. "That's what everyone calls you," Shea said. "That's what you want to be called."

Al forgot about being the perfect young lady for a moment. "Only because Alessandra is such a dorky name."

"No," Dottie considered. "It's not a dorky name. I think it's a beautiful name, but there's nothing wrong with a nickname."

She dropped her purse on the sofa as if she belonged there. Fitting in came easily to her, Shea thought. It was a talent he had cultivated himself when he was younger. Dottie appeared to do it effortlessly.

"What's yours?" Al asked.

Dottie sat on the arm of the sofa so that she could look into Al's face instead of down at it. "Dottie *is* my nickname. My real name is Dorothea."

Al wrinkled her nose. "That's even worse than Alessandra."

"I used to think so," Dottie agreed, "when I was your age."

Al took a step closer to the woman. "What else did you think when you were my age?"

Dottie grinned. "That adults didn't know anything."

Al flashed a smile. It was obviously something she was inclined to agree with. "But my Dad does and he's an adult."

Dottie smiled as she looked toward Shea. "Yes, he is." A very handsome adult, she added silently. "And he's smart enough to know that he might need a little help when it comes to introducing you to all the things a 'lady of breeding'—" Dottie raised her eyes to Shea before looking back at Al "—should know."

She saw the torn look that suddenly rose in the girl's eyes. "What's the matter?" she asked gently.

"Am I going to have to give up my softball games?"

The turmoil the girl was going through was evident in her voice. Dottie could remember a similar dilemma that had claimed her around the same age. "There isn't a reason in the world why you should give up something you love to do to achieve something else. I know lots of baseball players who are gentlemen. There's no reason why you can't be a lady and still play ball. You give me a schedule of your games and we'll work around them. How's that sound?"

"Terrific! I mean, okay, I guess." She cast a sidelong glance at her father. "Are we going to go to things like museums and ballets?"

"Yes," Dottie answered. "That's going to be part of it."

Suddenly, as though a little nervous, Al asked, "Can Daddy come along?"

Dottie smiled. A bonus. "Certainly Daddy can come. If he wants to."

Al turned her face up to Shea's. "Daddy?"

He hadn't bargained on this. "Well, I—" Shea began to hedge.

Al entwined her arms through his. The girl didn't need any lessons in manipulation, Dottie thought. She seemed to have that part down pat.

"C'mon, Dad, it'll be fun. Please?" Al pressed.

"I suppose it couldn't hurt." He looked at Dottie. "What did you have in mind?"

"Well, for openers, I thought we'd go to the L.A. County Museum of Art." She turned toward the girl. "Is that all right with you, Al?"

"It sounds wonderful."

But Dottie knew better. The answer had come too quickly and had been too forced. "If we're going to work together I think you'd better level with me."

Shea looked over Dottie's shoulder and said to Al, "She said the same thing to me."

Dottie kept her mind on Al, not on the man who had stirred her imagination all last night. "There's a 'but' in your voice."

"A 'but'?" Al echoed a little too innocently.

"Honesty is the hallmark of being a lady, Al," Dottie said, putting an arm around the girl's shoulders. "You're not really excited about having to go to a museum." She saw the surprise on Al's face at being so easily read. Dottie grinned. "What would you *really* like to do?"

"Well," Al dragged the word out, pretending to think when the answer was on the tip of her tongue. "Go to the zoo."

A girl after her own heart. "Sounds like a great idea. I tell you what, we'll divide the day. Half and half. How's that sound?"

"Exhausting," Shea commented.

"All right!" was Al's answer.

The light in Al's eyes told her everything. "This time, I believe you. The 'ayes' have it, Mr. Delany." Dottie turned to look at the man on her left. "I'm afraid you're outvoted."

"So it seems."

Why did he have the feeling that this was going to be par for the course?

Chapter Three

"**W**ow." Al's single exclamation was swallowed up by the vast walls of the Ahmanson Gallery, one of the five buildings that comprised the Los Angeles County Museum of Art. From where she stood, Al could see huge expansive rooms attached like wings to the central body on either side and an open staircase leading up to other floors. And they were all filled with paintings.

She turned toward Dottie, her bright green eyes full of wonder. And dismay. Al was obviously feeling overwhelmed before she even started. "Am I going to have to know everything?"

Shea laughed softly as Dottie shook her head in answer to the girl's question. "No one knows everything," she assured her.

"My mother did."

Dottie glanced at Shea and saw the set of his mouth harden. All right, how was she to respond to this, she wondered, temporarily at a loss. She certainly didn't want to drive any wedges between Al and the memory of her mother. And she didn't want to antagonize Shea. But Al obviously believed what she had just said, and trying to live up to an impossible standard would only reap trouble for the girl.

Iron fist, kid glove, Dottie reminded herself. "Did your grandmother tell you that?"

Al was still rather dazzled by the vastness of the museum. "Yes."

Dottie smiled. She had a way out. "Parents have a way of glorifying their children's accomplishments—when their children can't hear them. Within earshot, the praise usually gets a little thinner."

"Or nonexistent," Shea muttered, more to himself than to either of them. He was here for Al, he reminded himself, and to see how Dottie conducted herself as a teacher. He wasn't here to think about unpleasant topics, topics that always had a way of surfacing whenever he thought of Louisa.

Dottie waited for Shea to elaborate on his comment. But he was no longer looking in her direction. Instead, he had turned to the information desk to pick up a brochure on the museum.

Was he referring to himself as a parent? She watched him glance through the small pamphlet. No, what she had witnessed in his living room told her that Shea and his daughter had a good relationship. The kind that was based on love and lavish praise. What was he referring to then? His own childhood? His wife's?

There were a lot of things she realized that she wanted to know about Shea Delany and his world. She found it very difficult to curb her tongue and hold back her questions. She had always believed that if she wanted to know something, she went ahead and asked. But J.T. had already warned her that Shea was not a man who shared things easily. And he had confirmed as much in the restaurant. It was going to take her a while before she could get him to trust her enough to open up. Until then, she was just going to have to be patient.

For now, there was Al and her own role as a female Rex Harrison. She turned to the girl. Al still appeared somewhat intimidated by the museum.

"You don't have to know everything. No one expects that," she told Al.

Shea had looked up from the pamphlet, trying to be discreet, but Dottie knew he was listening to her conversation with Al, evaluating her responses. His expression was unreadable. Was he judging her as a teacher, or something more? She couldn't help the little thrill of anticipation that zipped through her.

"And it doesn't happen overnight." Easily, Dottie took the brochure from Shea and paged through it, quickly deciding their itinerary for their first visit. "For the time being, let's just introduce you to some of the artists and their paintings." Taking Al by the arm, she drew her to the center of the foyer, where the wings met. "We'll get a feel for what you like."

Al stared at her. "What I like?"

The surprise in the girl's voice made Dottie smile. This was going to be fun. "Yes."

"Is that important?"

"Absolutely. Art appreciation means just what it says. Appreciating something means seeing its value, but it can also refer to liking something." She drew on something close to her. "You can appreciate the fact that Picasso was an innovative, inspired artist—but you don't have to like what he painted." She never had.

"I don't?"

He was still silently watching her, Dottie thought. Was she passing his test? She could only say what she believed, no matter what the outcome. Still, it would be nice to have him approve, not because he was paying her for this, but because of him. He was the type of man she had a feeling she should get to know and get to know well. That, she mused, was probably going to be a lot harder than teaching Al a few of the basic things she was striving to learn.

"Nope," Dottie answered cheerfully.

Al let out a sigh and looked greatly relieved. Dottie tried not to laugh. "Shall we get started?" Dottie suggested.

The girl looked on either side of her. "Which way?"

She could set a course, but she wanted to give Al the chance to make decisions. Confidence came from being able to make choices, and though she had a feeling that Al wasn't timid in the comfort of her own world, this was a new area she was entering. One step into the adult world.

"You choose." She gestured around. "There are paintings all over here."

Al raised her eyes to Dottie, still feeling her way around. "Left?"

Dottie slipped her arm through Al's and smiled at her encouragingly. "Left it is."

Shea fell into step at Dottie's other side. For the moment, he preferred not to have his daughter between them. As a teacher, this woman who had breezed into his life was rather unorthodox. But he liked that. Perhaps more than he felt he should. "A little unstructured, aren't you?"

She turned and grinned up into his face as they stepped into the left wing. The whimsical turn of her lips made him want to touch her, to gently move his thumb along her bottom lip just before he kissed her.

"A little," she agreed. "A lot if you ask certain members of my family. That's supposed to be part of my charm, Shea." She winked, then turned her attention back to Al.

Yes, he thought, following her, it was.

J.T. had been right. Dottie McClellan really did know art. For an hour and a half, she had been subtly leading his daughter from room to room, discussing the paintings as if they were living, breathing entities and the artists as if they were old friends who were likely to drop in on her at any moment. She took the dry dustiness out of knowledge, he thought, both amused and absorbed by her method. He wondered if her family had been the sort to take regular trips to museums and galleries and theaters.

A small, disparaging smile curved his lips as he thought of his own childhood. The only artwork he had ever seen when he was growing up was the graffiti on the buildings. He had fought for every bit of the sophistication he had now. Every layer had been hard won.

She had probably been born to it, he decided, born to breeding and wealth. He envied her the former. And wondered about her a great deal more than he knew he should.

Al was squinting uncertainly at the painting before her. It was a painting by El Greco, the figures thin and elongated. She turned to Dottie, bit her lower lip and pondered her own question before she asked, "Did he have an eye problem?" Looking back at the painting, she tilted her head and tried to get a different perspective on it.

During the tour, Shea had said very little. Dottie was very aware of his presence, even though her conversation was predominantly directed toward Al. Dottie wondered if he felt left out. She turned to him. "Do you want to answer that, or shall I?"

Shea raised an eyebrow in amusement. She'd make a good politician if she ever decided to run. "I'm just a tourist here." With a flourish of his hand, he gave her back the floor. "It's your class."

Dottie smiled at him, a bright, open smile that went directly into his nervous system, unsettling things that had long been dormant.

"That was very astute of you to pick that up, Al. Some people believe El Greco did." Al looked very pleased with herself at Dottie's praise. "That doesn't diminish the grandeur of his work, though." Dottie crossed her arms before her and studied the painting for a moment before turning back to Al. "Do you like it?"

Al glanced at Dottie as if to gauge what her response should be. "I think so."

"Some things take time." Dottie found herself looking at Shea for a second before continuing. She felt a small, insistent flutter in her stomach. "They grow on you slowly and you find yourself liking them more and more as time goes on. It's not always love at first sight."

Something rose in Shea's eyes at her words, then disappeared. Amusement? Recognition? She didn't know.

"When I first had to read Shakespeare, for instance, I thought it was just a bunch of jumbled up words that didn't make sense. It was pure torture for me." Dottie turned and they slowly drifted out of the room into the main foyer again. "I love it now."

"Why?" Al asked.

Yes, why? Shea echoed in his mind, waiting to hear her reasons. She was an intriguing box of surprises.

Dottie grinned, remembering the first time it had all come together for her. She had been a couple of years older than Al. It was during a semiprofessional production of *Henry IV, Part I.* Suddenly, in the mouths of the actors, the words had sprang to life. "For the majesty of the words. For the stories, the people in them, but mostly for the sound of the words."

She saw an empty marble bench against one of the walls and crossed to it. She sat in the middle, motioning Al to her. Shea remained standing.

"C'mon," Dottie urged, "there's room enough for three."

Because it was more awkward not to, Shea sat next to her. But he was closer to her than he wanted to be. She stirred him and he didn't want to be stirred, didn't want to be reminded of the things he was doing without. So he sat and thought of other things, and let her perfume seep into his system, rustling memories, rustling desires he'd thought had turned brown with age and blown away.

"All right, Al," Dottie began gamely, "which one did you like best?" The young girl stiffened slightly. Dottie smiled and gently placed her hand over Al's. "This isn't a quiz, Al. This is a conversation. Do you like any painting better than the others?"

"Yes," the girl said slowly.

Shea leaned forward to look at his daughter, curious. "Which one?"

"Ka—Kaminsky?" Al looked to Dottie for confirmation of the artist's name.

"Kandinsky?" Shea asked before Dottie could correct Al. He would have thought that Al's taste would run to one of the Romanticists. Or perhaps Turner's seascapes. Recognizable things. He would have never guessed that she'd pick an Expressionist.

Encouraged by the look on Dottie's face, Al answered, "Yes. That first one you showed me."

"Okay." Dottie nodded. "Why?"

Al seemed distressed. "Why?"

"Yes, why?" Dottie repeated. "People usually have reasons for liking one thing over another. What are yours?"

Al shrugged helplessly. "I don't have reasons."

Dottie wasn't about to let it go that easily. "Sure you do. You just haven't thought about them. Think about them now."

Impressed, Shea leaned back and waited to hear his daughter's answer.

"Well," Al drew out the word as she formed her thoughts. "I liked the colors."

"Good." Dottie nodded. "Why?"

Al was silent for a moment, thinking, her young face serious. "Because I could see things there." She brightened, going with her thoughts. "I can see whatever I want to see." She leaned toward Dottie, sharing a confidence. "I didn't see what he said I'd see, the artist I mean. His title didn't mean anything to me. I saw other images."

"Like an inkblot test?" Shea suggested, slightly amused.

Without thinking, Dottie poked him with her elbow, the way she did with Shad when he teased her. "Shh," she chided.

She had caught him totally off-guard. He had surrounded himself with sophisticated, subdued people for so long, he was completely unprepared for something as spontaneous as a playful poke in the ribs. It reminded him of another time and place. Of another lifetime ago when he had felt freer, even with poverty staring him in the face.

Al blinked, uncomprehending. "What's an inkblot test?"

"A lesson for another day," Dottie told her. "I like your answer."

Al grinned, looking pleased with herself. "You do?"

"Sure, it shows feeling, imagination." She put her arm around the girl. "There's nothing worse than following the herd blindly, parroting what they say. If you're following because you believe in the principles of the herd, that's great. But if you do it to be popular or because you're afraid to voice a contrary opinion or because you're too lazy to think things through, then it's bad.''

Al thought it over slowly. "Thinking's good, huh?''

Dottie rose. "Thinking's terrific.''

Al sprang to her feet, shifting from side to side next to Dottie. "Where do we go now?''

The only time he had seen Al looking that eager, Shea thought, was when she was getting ready to play in a ball game. He was pleasantly surprised and just a little sad at the fact that Al was growing up. She wasn't his little girl any more.

Dottie tucked away the brochure into her purse. "The zoo.''

For a moment, the newly attained cultured facade disappeared and Al's eyes lit up. But then she glanced around the foyer in dismay. "But we're not finished here.''

"We are for today. I don't want you to go on overload. After a while, everything starts to look alike.'' Al seemed a little frustrated. "Don't worry,'' Dottie assured her. "The museum will still be here on Monday.'' Al still looked unconvinced. "The trick in life, Al, is to carefully balance out everything. We've put in time 'working,' now we're ready to have some fun.'' She turned toward Shea. "Is that all right with you?''

Shea thought of the torturous midafternoon traffic he would be facing. "It'll be hell to get to the zoo this time of day.'' He saw the unspoken plea that suddenly came into Al's eyes. Shea relented. "But we'll give it a shot.'' Both Al and Dottie grinned their thanks, and to Shea, that made it worth the aggravation.

"I noticed a little coffee shop on the way over here. Why don't we stop for a bite to eat and then we can continue on the second leg of our odyssey?" Dottie suggested to him.

She was taking charge, he thought. Just like that. Effortlessly. How did she manage to do it?

"Odyssey?" Al repeated, drawing attention back to herself. "I thought we were going to the zoo."

Dottie laughed and placed her arm around the girl again, giving her a hug. "That, too."

Al smiled. Shea could see that she liked the woman he'd chosen. Dottie made things fun and didn't make Al feel foolish when she asked questions.

"What's an odyssey, Dottie?"

"A journey." Dottie smiled at him as she walked outside. "This is a journey into awareness."

Possibly, Shea thought, his eyes drifting over her form as she walked ahead of him, for more than one of them.

She should have worn jeans, Dottie thought, but jeans wouldn't have created the right first impression. She glanced down at her skirt. Grass stains creased the hem where she had knelt down to pet one of the animals. Would they ever come out? Still, it was worth it. She was having a wonderful time.

She jumped as a kid butted her. Shea grabbed her arm to steady her and pulled her toward him without thinking. There was the briefest of encounters, just a slight touching of bodies before Dottie had moved away. But it had been enough. Enough to tell her that she was right. Enough to warn him to keep his distance. Unexpectedly, heat had surged straight from her stomach, pouring through her suddenly taut breasts, her tingling limbs.

She flashed Shea a smile, wishing that he wasn't quite so overwhelmingly handsome, and turned her attention to Al.

The girl hadn't seen anything. She was occupied with several ducklings.

Dottie stooped to pet the duckling closest to her. "The petting zoo here has got to be one of my favorite places in the whole world."

Al looked at her in surprise. "You're kidding?"

Dottie carefully scooped up a duckling, gently stroking the downy feathers. "Do I look like I'm kidding?" The duckling uttered a complaint, then squirmed out of Dottie's hands, waddling off indignantly.

Shea laughed and took Dottie's hand to help her to her feet. The contact felt warm and pleasing. And arousing. It mystified him even as it pulled at him. "No, you look very serious," he commented.

"I am." She brushed off her knees and saw that Shea was watching her. The fact created a warm blush that spread inside of her.

"But you're a lady, aren't you?" Al seemed thoroughly confused.

Time for a definition. Dottie placed her hands on Al's shoulders. "A lady is many things, Al. Being one doesn't mean long gowns, endless accomplishments and a passion for classical music. Being a lady is what you are inside. It means being kind and thoughtful. I've known ladies in rags and very unladylike women in designer clothes. C'mon," she urged, "let's go see the koalas."

Shea shook his head as he walked next to her. "When did you know ladies in rags?" He kept his voice low so Al wouldn't hear.

Dottie grinned, a mischievous sparkle in her eyes. He had caught her. "I thought it made a nice touch," she answered, her voice as low as his. "Not rags, exactly, just not very expensive clothes. Housedresses, mostly." It was her foster mother she had been thinking of. The Marinos had not been well off when she and Shad had first come to live with them. The money came later, after Salvatore Marino had made a go of his tile business. But money made no difference. She knew of no finer lady than Bridgette Marino. "Sometimes, a little imagery helps."

Yes, the right image did help. It made things more vivid. *She* made things more vivid. In the space of one day, she had brought new life and breath into stale, dry subjects. She had a fresh way of looking at things that made him see as if for the first time. Shea was beginning to feel that he was getting as much out of this in his own way as Al was.

Just as long as he didn't get more than he bargained for.

He was glad that J.T. had coaxed the matter out of him. He was even happier that Dottie hadn't listened to him in the restaurant when he had changed his mind about the practicality of all this. He'd been right about a woman making things easier for Al. He had thought more in terms of questions that Al might have been too embarrassed to ask him about. Women things. He had no idea that Dottie would be this good. Al had certainly taken to her quickly.

And so, perhaps, had he. But that was beside the point. It seemed that Dottie McClellan had a lot to offer his daughter. That she was very easy on the eye didn't hurt either, although he knew that in the long run, things like that didn't really matter. Not to him. He had no time for involvements, and, if he were honest with himself, no courage for them either. Not after the last time.

"Too bad we didn't bring a camera," Dottie commented as they approached the cage where the koalas were kept. "They really are adorable." They looked so much like live teddy bears, she wanted to reach out and touch one. "Oh well, maybe next time."

"Next time?" Al looked at her hopefully.

Dottie turned from the cage, backing into Shea. She took a step to the side, though the impression of his body against hers lingered. "Sure. I come here whenever I can. We can plan to do this again, if you like," she offered. "It's going to be a long summer."

Shea watched Al's grin spread from ear to ear as she forgot to be the budding young lady she was aspiring to become. "Neat."

"Yeah," Dottie agreed, tucking her arm around the girl's shoulders. "Neat." They turned a corner, walking toward the elephants' compound.

"Yes," Al corrected hesitantly.

Dottie looked at her, confused. "Yes, what?"

Al shook her head vigorously, her hair bouncing about her face. "My dad said you shouldn't say 'yeah.'" She looked to her father for encouragement. "You should say 'yes.' A lady always says 'yes.'"

"Does she, now?" Dottie looked at Shea, an amused smile on her face. He knew without asking that she was reading another meaning into his innocent words. Her eyes were laughing at him, teasing him. She had beautiful eyes, eyes that haunted him even as they penetrated his system.

Dottie laughed. "Well, I'm off duty now. So an occasional 'yeah' is all right."

"Can you do that?" Al questioned her.

"Do what?"

"Go off duty?"

"Sure." Dottie took her hand as they resumed walking. "Remember, it's not something you have to work at all the time, it's just something you are."

Shea liked her philosophy. "So don't try too hard," he chimed in. "Relax."

Dottie nodded at his choice of words. "Being relaxed is very important," she agreed. She turned to Shea. "Banana?"

Shea stared at her. What was she talking about? "Excuse me?"

"Frozen chocolate covered bananas." Dottie pointed to the stand at the end of the path. There was amusement in her eyes. "My treat. Any takers?"

"Sure." Al shifted from foot to foot.

Dottie turned to Shea, waiting for his answer. Shea nodded. "Why not?"

"Why not, indeed?"

Why did he get this feeling that there were some sort of hidden messages beneath her words? She wasn't the devious type, at least he didn't think so. Maybe he was just reading things into the way she turned a phrase and the tone she used at times. It was as if she was telling him to leave the realm where he had dwelled for the last six years and rejoin the living.

He was imagining things.

He watched as Dottie paid the vendor for three chocolate covered bananas. She handed one to Al and one to him, then took the remaining one for herself. Pulling off the wrapper, she bit into it the way she apparently bit into life, Shea observed. With gusto.

"This is fun, Dottie," Al said as they walked down a shaded path. The sign above them pointed to the monkey exhibit.

She was glad that Al was enjoying herself and that this was going so well. Dottie sneaked a glance at Shea. Very well. "Life should be fun," Dottie pointed out.

But it wasn't, Shea thought. It was cruel. Just as you get everything you want, life pulled a rug out from under you, slammed a door, destroyed a dream.

Al seemed unaware of the pensive look on her father's face, but Dottie wasn't. What was he thinking about?

"Grandmother thinks that life should be full of lessons."

Grandmother, Dottie was beginning to think, sounded like a cross between Queen Victoria and a harpy. It was becoming evident why Shea's voice had been frosty when he had mentioned the woman to her yesterday. "Maybe, but the lessons don't have to be boring. You just need the right teacher."

"Like you," Shea said.

The compliment surprised and pleased her. Dottie grinned. "Like me."

There was no conceit in the words, Shea noticed. She was stating a fact she believed in. Was she really as self-assured, as confident as she portrayed herself? If she was, she was a very rare woman. He thought of Sandra, of her insecurities, of her inability to make decisions. Of her fear of displeasing her mother. She would have done well to have had someone like Dottie in her life, helping to bolster her. In seeking to help, he had only managed to make a mess of her life.

"You're melting," Dottie said suddenly.

The fog lifting from his mind, he looked at her dumbly. "What?"

Dottie pointed to the chocolate around the banana. It was dripping down his fingers and onto his shirt. "The chocolate, it's melting."

Without thinking, she reached for a napkin and began to rub at the dark stain on his shirt. The action was swift, simple and yet the sweet intimacy of it jolted them both. She felt the muscular ridge beneath her fingers rise and fall, absorbed the beat of his heart as it increased.

Dottie looked up into his eyes, something warm and beckoning coursing through her. Interesting, she thought. Very interesting. And very nice.

"Here." She handed the napkin to him. "There's a fountain over there. Maybe you'd better finish that yourself."

He took the napkin from her, working hard to rein in sensations that had surfaced, red-hot and disturbing. "Yes, maybe I'd better."

Chapter Four

Shea had had no idea when he had made the financial arrangements with Dottie, that he would be getting so much for his money. Her car was still there as he pulled into his driveway, just as it had been every night this week.

He remembered that J.T. had told him, while listing her sister-in-law's qualifications, that Dottie had a tendency to throw herself into whatever she was doing.

Well, he thought, getting out of the car, she had certainly "thrown" herself into this. With very gratifying results. He was having some very interesting conversations with Al these days, conversations that no longer revolved around the animal kingdom or the most recent trades of baseball players.

A bittersweet smile lifted his lips. In a way, he rather missed that.

He unlocked the front door and walked into the house to the sound of high-pitched, female laughter. Athena materialized to his left and nodded, as if reading his mind.

"It has been going on like that all afternoon." She shook her head as she wiped her hands on the crisp white apron tied around her waist. "Learning certainly seems to make that child happy."

He dropped his briefcase next to the elegant nineteenth-century writing desk he had lovingly and painstakingly restored. It had been a gift for Sandra on their first anniversary. He enjoyed restoring things, bringing out their hidden beauty. In a way, it was like reliving the process he himself had gone through in his fight to triumph over circumstances. "There are worse things."

Athena studied him for a moment. "Yes, like a man who will not stop mourning what is lost and gone."

Shea gave her a warning look. Athena lifted her head slightly. Frustrated annoyance creased her brow as she held her tongue. For now. Shea knew the stay was only temporary. She would say something again. And again. Though she had worked for Sandra's family first, Athena's loyalty was now to Al. And to him.

He heard Al giggle again and his expression softened. "Dinner ready?"

"Yes." Athena looked off in the direction of the living room. "She will not stay."

"Dottie?" It was a rhetorical question.

Athena nodded, clearly annoyed at having her plans thwarted. "A perfectly good meal and she says she must go home." She gestured majestically toward the living room. "See what you can do with her."

Shea merely laughed. "If the woman wants to go home, there's nothing I can do."

Athena stopped, her back against the swinging kitchen door. "Ah, there you are wrong, Mr. Shea. I think there is much you can do with this woman. The trick," she smiled pointedly at him, "is the wanting to."

He had had enough of this conversation. "Athena, our dinner is calling you."

For now, she would be dismissed. But it was evident from her manner that the topic was not settled. "And opportunity is finally calling you. I would heed it if I were you." She turned and disappeared into the kitchen. The door swung shut behind her.

"Lucky for me, you're not," he muttered as he walked into the living room.

Dottie looked up as Shea crossed the threshold. She had heard the car pull into the driveway, heard him speaking to Athena, and though she never lost the thread of what she was saying to Al, she had been waiting for him to enter.

The light tan suit fit him well, as if it were made just for him. It probably was. In it, he cast an aura of the successful, sophisticated cosmopolitan man. But there was another aura she detected. A far more rugged one. He made her think of a dark-haired, James Dean type. A rebel *with* a cause.

She smiled at the image it created in her mind. She could see him like that, slightly ruthless, with an air of danger about him. Dangerous, that was the word that best described him. Beneath the polished manners and smooth words, there was definitely something dangerous. She felt a shaft of excitement sail swiftly through her.

Shifting, Dottie closed the huge book on modern artists that she held in her lap. "Your dad's here," she said needlessly. "That's it for today." Al was already on her feet.

"Hi, Dad." Al rose up on her toes and brushed a fleeting kiss on her father's cheek. "I've got to call Jessi before dinner." With that, she dashed from the room, leaving them alone together.

As if by design. Shea couldn't help wondering if Athena had been talking to Al.

"So." He dropped into the Victorian walnut armchair that faced the sofa. "How's it going?"

"Beautifully, I would say." Carefully, she placed the book on the coffee table, wondering if the fragile-looking legs could support the heavy tome. Antiques always made her nervous. She could never tell if they were strong enough to withstand the stress of daily living. *Her* daily living. "She's really soaking it up."

Her eyes looked green to him in this light. They reflected the color of her sweater. A sweater that made him very aware of just how much of a woman she was. To blot out the impression, he looked off in the direction his daughter had taken. "As long as she's happy."

Dottie leaned over and reached for her purse, which was lying on the floor next to the sofa. "That means a lot to you, doesn't it?"

He looked at her, surprised at her question. "I wouldn't think you'd have to ask."

No, she didn't. She was just making casual conversation because she sensed his discomfort. With what, she wasn't certain. "Reinforcement's always a good thing." She started to leave, then stopped. "Oh, by the way." She pulled out a white envelope from her purse and handed him three tickets. "Here."

As he looked down at the tickets in his hand, his hair fell into his eyes, making him look roguishly boyish. Dottie suppressed the urge to brush it aside for him. "What's this?"

"Tickets."

His eyes narrowed. "To what?"

She took them out of the envelope and held them up. *"Fiddler on the Roof.* It's playing at the Performing Arts Center."

Shea read the date stamped on them. "They're for tomorrow night."

"Yes, I know." She saw a trace of annoyance cross his face. "They're all sold out, but I have an in with someone on the board of directors."

Yes, he'd imagined that she would. He could see her having an in with a lot of people, flitting in and out of their lives like a warm summer wind. She didn't seem like the type to be hampered by formalities and barriers. He had learned that already. That still didn't give her the right to make plans for him. "That's not what I meant."

She waited patiently. "What did you mean?"

"This is short notice." He looked down at her face and wondered why he wanted her so much when other women, far more stunningly beautiful, had floated through his life, available and willing. He had felt nothing for any of them, had wanted nothing. Dottie made him remember what wanting was. "Did you ever think of asking if I was going to be busy?"

"I did." He raised his eyebrows in response. "I asked Al. She said you usually stay home on Saturdays and watch videos with her."

His daughter had taken a little of the thunder away from his stand. "Usually, but not always."

"I took a chance." A slender shoulder rose and fell but he detected no chagrin on her part. "*Are* you busy tomorrow night?"

"No."

She could see that the admission annoyed him. She smiled to herself. "Then it's lucky I got the tickets, isn't it? Would you mind picking me up at seven? I live closer to the Performing Arts Center than you do and this way we won't be inconvenienced by having to have two cars parked."

There was no point in being put out with her. She didn't seem to notice when he was. "I will if you answer a question."

She tilted her head back, an easy smile on her lips. "Anything."

He wondered if he could hold her to that. And what she would do if he kissed her. Kiss back, probably. It made it all the more difficult to curb his desire. "Do you always come on like a commando?"

Her purse slipped off her shoulder and she tugged it back up. "I wasn't aware that I was. Of course my brothers probably think I do, but you know how brothers are."

"No," he answered truthfully, "I don't."

A tiny wedge into the past had opened up. She was quick to make use of the opportunity. "Were you an only child?"

But he was quicker. A small smile quirked his lips in amusement. "Practicing your trade?"

"No, asking questions," she replied innocently. She wished that he'd relax and open up a little. She'd known him a week and didn't know much more than what J.T. had told her about Shea. It wasn't the way things normally went. Within a week, she usually had a complete bio on a person, if they mattered to her. And he did. "It's what I do best, I'm told."

He had a feeling that there were other things she did equally well, if not better.

"If you two are going to continue talking," Athena announced from the dining room doorway, her hands on her hips, "you can do it over dinner." She looked at Shea accusingly. "It is growing cold."

"I think that's my cue." Dottie turned and took a couple of steps toward the door. "I have to go home and feed the menagerie."

Was that the way she referred to her family? It would be in keeping with her unorthodox personality. He hadn't bothered to ask J.T. if Dottie were married. It hadn't mattered a week ago.

It shouldn't matter now. But it did. He glanced at her left hand. It was bare.

She saw what he was looking at. "My pets," she clarified. It sounded better than declaring that she wasn't married. He'd think that she was eager and she wasn't. At least, not for marriage for its own sake.

There was no reason in the world why her explanation should have made the slightest difference in the way he viewed the rest of the evening. But a lightness suddenly wafted through him that he could only honestly recognize as relief.

"Mr. Shea." Athena's voice was authoritative and demanding.

"She does crack a whip, doesn't she?" Dottie laughed as she crossed to the front door. "'Bye, Athena." The woman nodded in her direction, her solemn expression unchanged. Dottie turned and looked at Shea once more before she left. "See you tomorrow night."

He nodded. "At seven."

Seven, she mouthed in response, then closed the door behind her. He turned around. Athena was still standing there, her lips pursed in disapproval.

"You are out of practice, Mr. Shea." She shook her head in dismay.

"At what?"

"Living," was all she said as she turned on her heel and stalked back into the kitchen.

As he surrendered his white car to the valet, Shea wondered how far back from the stage their seats were. When he drew the tickets out again to present to the usher, he read the location for the first time. Third row, center.

Shea looked at Dottie in surprise as the usher preceded them down the aisle. "I thought you said the performance was sold out."

"It is."

Shea guided Al in front of him as they moved down the aisle. "Then how did you manage to get seats this good?"

She glanced over her shoulder, her sheer blue scarf shimmering on her bare skin. "I told you, I have an in with one of the directors."

He couldn't help wondering just what that "in" included. Was she just friendly with the man? Or was it something more? He felt another pang of emotion stirring within him that he refused to acknowledge.

"What did he ask for in trade?" He stopped as the usher stood off to one side, allowing them to be seated.

Dottie went first, carefully making her way down the row to her seat. She could have sworn she had heard a tinge of jealousy in his voice even though he had kept his expression blank.

Dottie waited until they were all seated before she answered. "That I help her son find a good printer for his computer."

"Her? The director's a woman?" He could have bitten his tongue off for that.

He *was* jealous. The thought warmed her. "Women can sit on the board of directors." She looked at Al who had taken the seat between then. "Right, Al?"

"Right." Al gave her father a superior look, enjoying this camaraderie with Dottie.

"I never said they couldn't." Shea didn't bother to keep the smile from his lips.

* * *

The performance was superb. He had to admit that he couldn't have chosen a better introduction into the world of theater for Al. Each time he glanced at her during the evening, her eyes were riveted to the stage, a rapturous expression on her face.

As Tevye bid his second daughter goodbye on the steps of the train depot, Shea saw tears sliding down Al's cheek. He was about to comfort her when he caught Dottie's eye over the girl's head. Dottie shook her head slightly, indicating that he shouldn't say anything. This was all part of the awakening experience for Al and she didn't want the young girl embarrassed about it until she had grown comfortable with her feelings. Tomboys felt that it was a weakness to display tears unless they were knocked down stealing home plate.

Shea shrugged and turned his attention back to the stage. Despite the tuneful music and clear voices that swelled throughout every corner of the theater, his mind was only partially on the play taking place before him. Here, in the huge darkened theater that was filled to capacity with elegantly clothed men and women, he was aware of the fact that he could only sense her presence.

With all the different perfumes and colognes that had to have been worn tonight, he could only catch the musky, seductive scent of hers. It was as if he had absolutely no control over the matter, no ability to resist.

This was what was called chemistry, he supposed. Once he had been a great believer in chemistry, using it to his advantage, both in his business dealings and in his encounters with women. If there were consequences, he found a way around them. Always. He had let his hormones take him where they would, enjoying one willing partner after another, no strings, no promises, pleasure with an end in sight. Until Sandra.

Sandra brought culture into his life that he had only feigned having before. Sandra, with her heritage that went back to the founding fathers, Sandra with her gentle humor, her timid ways and her large, soulful eyes. Sandra had changed everything for him, made him *become* what he had only pretended to be.

But he had destroyed what he had loved, destroyed because he *had* loved, and he had vowed that he would never let it happen again.

It had occurred a lifetime ago. Two lifetimes ago.

And now here *she* was, stirring him just by sitting a seat away, making him yearn, making him want, bringing it all back to him tenfold.

This was all just a purely routine physical reaction, he told himself, except that he no longer had them. These reactions, these demands that were suddenly swirling inside of him at a moment's notice were neither routine nor purely physical.

Dottie carefully leaned over behind Al, who sat on the edge of her seat, eagerly absorbing everything on stage. Her scent filled his head. "Aren't you enjoying this?"

Shea didn't turn to look at her. "Yes." His voice was tight.

Something *was* wrong. "You don't sound as if you're enjoying it."

Even in the dark theater she saw his eyes as he turned toward her. For a second, though she couldn't explain why, her heart stopped, then fluttered madly.

"Yes," she whispered, answering something she saw there. "Me, too."

He looked at her, wanting her to explain, but she had looked away. Shea gripped his program and stared at the actors on the stage.

Al didn't stop talking about the play the entire trip home. With only a few pointed questions from Dottie, Al expounded on the dances, the customs portrayed and the tiny bit of history that the play encompassed. She talked about everything and anything. That set a new record, Shea thought, even for her.

Al hugged the colored souvenir program that her father had bought her. "I always thought having people stop and break into song was sooo dumb." She beamed at Dottie. "I didn't know it could be so great."

Dottie had spent the entire ride sitting at an angle so that she could give Al her full attention. Her neck was beginning to ache. But it also afforded her a constant view of Shea's profile without being obvious. She watched moonlight play softly along the planes and angles of his face. Some things were worth the pain. "That's because the songs have a purpose. They tell you what the people are feeling. They're like soliloquies in Shakespeare."

Al made a face. "Shakespeare again?"

"No," Dottie corrected. "Shakespeare for the first time— next week."

Shea glanced at her. "More tickets?"

"More tickets." Dottie grinned.

Al groaned.

Dottie leaned her arm on the back of the seat and looked at the girl. "Remember what you just said you thought of musicals."

"Is Shakespeare going to be like that?"

"Even better—in time." Dottie turned around as Shea brought the car to a stop and put on the brake. "This isn't my house."

"No, it's mine." He opened the door on his side. "It's late," he explained as he got out. "I thought we'd drop Al off first." Logically, he knew he should have done it the other way around. But he wasn't thinking quite logically tonight. Not any more.

Al looked at Dottie and pouted. "But I'm not tired, Dad."

"It's eleven o'clock. You're tired." He opened her door, waiting.

Reluctantly, Al got out. "I want to go on talking about the play with Dottie."

"You," he assured her fondly, taking her arm, "will always go on talking. C'mon," he turned toward the front door, "let's tell Athena you're back."

Al looked over her shoulder at Dottie. "Are you coming, too?"

"No." Dottie winced as she massaged the crick in her neck. "I think I'll wait right here." She watched thoughtfully as Shea took his daughter into the house.

"Athena," he called as he walked in. "Athena, I'm going out for a while."

Athena appeared at the top of the stairs, her small, trim body swaddled in a flowing scarlet robe. "You have not gotten in yet." She joined Al at the foot of the stairs. "And just where is it you are going so late?"

He didn't like his affairs questioned. But he had gotten used to Athena's ways. There was affection behind them. "I'm taking Dottie home."

Athena's perfect teeth flashed in a wide smile. "I see."

Shea turned at the front door. "No, you don't see."

Athena shook her head at his tone of voice. Stubborn. "Then I am having better visions than you, Mr. Shea." She gestured him out over the threshold, then took hold of the doorknob. "I will see you in the morning."

Shea shook his head as the door closed behind him. His own mother had never shown this much concern about what he did. He glanced toward the car and saw Dottie still sitting in the passenger seat.

Or what he didn't do, he thought.

Dottie saw the pensive look as he drew near. "Something wrong?"

"No, I was just thinking." Shea closed the door as he slid behind the steering wheel. "If all Jamaican women are like Athena, it's a wonder there are any marriages on the island at all."

Dottie was prudent enough not to ask him what Athena had said to set him off. She instinctively knew that it was about them. She had seen the way the older woman had eyed the two of them last night when she had stood in the living room doorway.

Dottie hid her smile. "I like her."

Shea sighed and turned on the ignition. "Yeah, so do I."

Now she grinned, remembering what Al had said to her the other day. "If Al were here, she'd correct you. You said 'yeah,'" she explained in answer to his puzzled look. "Is it true all ladies always say yes?"

She had no doubts that they did, at least where Shea was concerned. J.T. had given her just the sketchiest background on his wife's death, but that had been six years ago. Dottie was surprised that someone as darkly good-looking as Shea was not surrounded with available women all vying for his attention.

He laughed. "I was just trying to teach her a little proper grammar."

"She's a very level-headed young girl." Dottie watched shadows chase each other across the hood of the car as he drove. "You seem to have taught her a lot of good things."

"Her grandmother would undoubtedly disagree with you there."

His expression was dark as he said the words. Dottie wanted to ask him about it, about what there was between him and the other woman. She sensed that there was a lot more to it than the usual in-law animosity. But now wasn't the time to ask. Yet.

Chapter Five

Dottie watched the distant silhouette of her house grow larger as Shea drove down her street. She turned toward him when he brought the car to a stop at the curb. "Would you like to come in?"

Shea knew he shouldn't, that whatever he had been feeling all evening would only intensify if he walked into her house now and was alone with her. The only intelligent thing to do would be to just say no, tell Dottie good-night and drive home as if the very devil was after him.

He'd always prided himself on doing the intelligent thing.

Shea pocketed his car keys and stared straight ahead for a moment. Something small and dark darted down the street. A black cat. It figured. "Yes."

"Terrific." She was already getting out of the car, her house key in hand.

Terrific? Was it? he wondered as he got out and followed her to her door. He doubted it very much. Yet he couldn't force himself to turn back. Not yet. Maybe he was facing up to his private demons. Or maybe he was just curious about his reactions to her and where they would lead. Whatever it was, he was here.

Dottie put the key into the lock and turned it. "I think I should warn you, though," she began as she started to push the door open.

"Warn me about what?" Suddenly, as they stepped inside, they were both engulfed in a flurry of fluff, fur, wet tongues and barking. Four dogs of various sizes, from a Great Dane to something he couldn't begin to properly identify, bounded at them from all sides, all vying for attention. Hers. Him they sniffed at curiously.

"That." Dottie laughed at the startled expression on his face.

Shea was quick to recover. "Your menagerie?" He moved as the Great Dane stepped in front of him.

"My menagerie." She stooped to scratch the dog closest to her. It was the little one of unknown origin. It could have doubled as a dust mop with eyes.

At least, Shea surmised those were eyes beneath the fur. He couldn't be sure. Maybe they were on the other end. It was hard to tell. The dog began to wiggle madly as soon as it came in contact with Dottie.

He could see how that could happen.

With the white dust mop in her arms, Dottie led the way into the kitchen. "This'll only take a minute." She picked up two of the four bowls from the floor and poured fresh water into them. "Down you go, Waldo." The dust mop leaped to the kitchen floor and waited, along with the others, while Dottie placed the bowls in front of them. "My brothers like to tease me about my pets." She refilled the other two bowls.

Shea looked around a little uncertainly, wondering if he should brace himself for another onslaught. "Are there any more around?"

"Pets?" She pulled a paper towel from the rack to her left and dried her fingers. "Just a couple of parakeets in the family room. Oh, and Howard."

Shea eyed the kitchen entrance for Howard. Obviously he was the sluggish one of the bunch. "A cat?"

"Here?" She tried to picture a cat surviving amid the four dogs for more than five minutes and couldn't. "Hardly." Carefully, she edged the Great Dane back, keeping the dog from monopolizing the area. The dust mop took advantage of the opening, secured a bowl and began lapping up water furiously. "No, Howard is a—"

Shea turned only to see a short, squat, dark animal come shuffling into the kitchen. "Pig?" He stared at it, and then at Dottie. She kept a *pig* in her house?

Maybe this was a little too much to spring on him at once. "A Vietnamese pot belly pig to be exact. Actually, Howard would rather think of himself as a member of the family. We don't use the 'p' word around him. He's very sensitive." She stooped to pat him affectionately.

Shea could have sworn that the animal brushed up against her leg like a cat. "How can you tell?"

"I just can," she said matter-of-factly. Rising, she decided that perhaps Shea had had enough of animal farm for the night. She moved Howard aside gently. "Would you like a nightcap?"

He looked down at the pig, who appeared to be contemplating the edibility of his shoes. Shea moved away slowly, not wanting to make the proverbial "wrong" move. "Please." He definitely needed one after this.

She laughed softly at his distress. "Howard is harmless." Taking Shea by the hand, she crossed a short hall to the living room. The entourage began to follow.

"I don't think we're alone," Shea pointed out as he looked over his shoulder.

Dottie glanced back. "Stay," she ordered in a stern voice that surprised him. It somehow seemed out of character for her. Obviously there was more to her than met the eye.

To his utter amazement, the animals obeyed. "That's incredible."

The smile she flashed was quick, guileless and infectious. "Just good training." She gestured toward the floral sofa. "Why don't you sit down?"

He cast a doubtful eye toward the kitchen, expecting the dogs or the pig, or all five to come bounding over at any moment. "Sure it's safe?"

"Absolutely." She qualified her statement by adding, "The animals won't bother you."

I might, of course, she thought as she opened up the small liquor cabinet against the far wall. He did look devastatingly handsome tonight.

Every night, she amended.

Shea noted the sofa as he sat down. Occupational habit, he thought. The piece belonged to no particular period, just standard department store furniture—comfortable, sagging a little like a worn old friend as it welcomed him. It had obviously seen a lot of use, though it looked sturdy enough.

Dottie turned, holding a half-filled bottle aloft. "Red wine all right?"

"Anything." Shea kept a tentative eye on the entrance to the living room.

Dottie laughed. Shea was obviously a little unnerved by her pets. She filled two long-stemmed glasses. People were usually put off by Howard until they got to know him. Of all her animals, he was the most docile and possibly the most loving and loyal.

She turned, a glass in each hand, and crossed to him. "Isn't it a little unusual, having a pig?" He accepted his glass.

Dottie lifted hers to her lips and took a sip. She liked the way light was trapped within the ruby liquid, making it shine.

"Probably. I read an article about them last year and went to a store that specialized in exotic pets to see for myself." She smiled fondly as she remembered. "Howard was the runt of the litter." She took another sip. "He needed me."

It was as simple as that, wasn't it? Shea realized. She felt needed, so she gave. She really was an incredible woman.

Dottie looked at Shea but he was glancing at the doorway again. Not even a single furry paw was evident. They stayed where she told them. "They've been given a bad rap, you know. Pigs. They don't really like to wallow in mud."

It seemed an odd thing to champion, he thought. "All the photographs I've ever seen of pigs, they're always in it."

She shook her head. Another soul in need of educating. "That's because people put them in mud. What would you do if someone put you in mud?"

He hated being dirty. It reminded him of of where he came from. "Take a shower."

She laughed. It was a simple enough answer. "So, what do you think?" She gestured around the room.

He looked, seeing it with a professional eye. While everything blended in nicely, it was never going to make the cover of any magazine. "It's—interesting."

She knew he was being polite. But she would bet that there was still a part of him that remembered what it was like, coming up from poverty. He wouldn't be an elitist.

"Well, my furniture doesn't have an alias, but it's comfortable." Dottie sank down next to him and the sofa sighed a little more.

Six inches wasn't nearly enough room to dissipate the warmth generated by her body. Six inches wasn't enough room for him to ignore his own reaction. "Excuse me?"

She played with the stem of her glass, watching the light bob and shimmer on top of the remaining liquid. "Where did I lose you?"

At the door. "'Alias'?"

She grinned, her lips spreading wide, and he wanted to kiss each corner slowly to savor the taste before he plunged in farther.

"My sofa isn't a Louis the Fourteenth. My coffee table only graced my foster mother's house, not some estate's." She leaned forward to tap it. It was a large, rectangular table with nicks and scratches that were discernible beneath a finely applied layer of varnish and lemon polish. It looked as if it could have withstood an elephant standing on it.

Or an affectionate pig, he thought.

"Nothing in here is a Chippendale, or from the Victorian era. It's all comfortable." She leaned back, a toss of her head sending her hair fanning out over her shoulder. "Just very comfortable."

Like its owner. She was comfortable. And exciting. At the same time. He found that intriguing even as he found it worrisome.

Suddenly aware of the glass in his hand, Shea took a long sip of his wine and let the liquid wind down slowly through his system, heating it. It was a tactical mistake. The wine only seemed to heighten his awareness. Of her. Of the way she moved, shifting, as she sat beside him. Of the fact that her strapless dress rustled against her as she breathed. And separated ever so slightly from her breasts when she exhaled.

The simple, blue brocade dress with its bustier top tempted him. Because he was a gentleman, he curbed the almost overwhelming urge he had to slowly peel the dress away from her supple body and glide his hands along her skin in its place.

Because he was a man, he wanted to.

Shea cleared his throat, afraid that he was being too obvious in the way he was looking at her. "You know, Al would be in heaven here."

Dottie could feel something developing between them. An electrical charge building up before the storm that was to come. She leaned her elbow against the cushion behind her, her face turned up to his. "She's welcome to come over any time." Her eyes moved to his mouth. A strong mouth. A sensual mouth. Her pulse quickened. "Tomorrow if you'd like." She placed her half-empty glass on the coffee table. Her hand trembled just a little.

Her dress dipped invitingly. Shea almost snapped the stem of his glass. "What I'd like—"

She saw something flicker in his eyes. Desire. And sorrow? "Yes?"

"Oh, the hell with it." Shea put down his drink so firmly that a little of the liquid sloshed up and down the side of the glass. He didn't notice as he took hold of her shoulders.

"I've never heard it put quite that romantically before," she laughed softly as his mouth drew close to hers.

And then she didn't laugh at all. There was no room for laughter, no room for light words. No lightness at all, except, perhaps in her head.

Ever since she had seen him in the restaurant, Dottie had wondered what it would be like to kiss Shea. Exciting. Dangerous. Romantic. None of her musings came within a mile of what she was experiencing now. His mouth was hot, demanding, drawing something from her that she had no idea, before this very moment, even existed. She could only liken it to an explosion. The kind that happened when universes were formed and planets and stars shot out into the heavens.

If once she had wondered if there would be passion, now she knew. There was. Reams of it. Oceans of it, so overwhelming that she was drowning, with absolutely no idea how to save herself. Or even the slightest inclination to do so.

Unconsciously, her arms tightened around his neck as she went with the sensations erupting within her.

It was like riding a bicycle; you never forgot. But Shea didn't quite remember it either, not like this. Sandra had always been sweet, but timid in her lovemaking. He had almost been afraid of shattering her, she was so fragile. She had been soft, small, delicate, capable of love. But she had never stirred this within him. He had never felt this power that left his knees weak. The women who had come before Sandra were faceless, meaningless, pleasures long forgotten and not missed.

This was something else again. This was like getting sucked into a black hole in space. No bottom, no end, fear and excitement riding along the perimeter. He felt exhilarated. Alive.

And scared as hell.

She felt soft in his hands, soft, yet sturdy. There was a subtle strength in this woman despite the lighthearted way she moved through life. No one was ever going to make her do or say anything she didn't want to. He could respect a woman like that, admire a woman like that.

Perhaps even love a woman like that.

But he couldn't love her. He couldn't, shouldn't, love at all. He'd seen the destructive powers of love firsthand. He was guilty, had blood on his hands because of it, and he vowed that it would never, ever happen again. He would never be the cause of another person's ruin. He carried that burden with him always. He wasn't fit to have another love come his way.

She felt the change the moment it occurred. One moment, there was a tidal wave of passion, of desire, flowing over both of them. And then, just before all thoughts vanished, burnt away by the incredible heat rising through her entire body, he was suddenly drawing away, ending the kiss before it had fully begun.

Why?

Her lips felt cold, numbed by the air that hit them as his mouth left hers. Dottie blinked, trying desperately to reorient herself. She drew a deep breath, wanting to steady herself before she spoke. "Was it something I said?"

This was insane. How had he let himself go like that? Shea struggled for composure. He felt dazed, confused. Her question took a second to fully register. "What?"

Dottie lifted her chin, as if that would help steady her pulse. "You stopped."

She was so simply direct, it was hard not to answer. "It was either that, or die from lack of oxygen." He realized that his tie was askew. So was the rest of him, probably. Shea straightened his tie. The rest would be harder to fix.

His answer didn't fool her. She knew body language well enough. "What are we going to do about this?"

He looked at her blankly. What was she suggesting? "Do?"

Dottie folded her hands in her lap and looked at him directly. Something was happening here and she wasn't about to shrug it off. Or lose it before she understood it. "That wasn't exactly a thank-you-very-much-for-the-free-tickets-good-night kiss.''

He raised one eyebrow. His intention was to be slightly sarcastic to chase her off the trail. ''You've had experience.''

His intent failed in the face of her answer. ''Nothing like what just happened.''

He resisted cupping her face in his hand and kissing her again. ''Dottie, I think I'd better go.'' He rose decisively to his feet.

She looked up at him, trying to fathom what was going on in his mind. ''Forever?''

Shea looked at her. She kept cutting through things too astutely. ''What?''

Slowly, she searched along the floor with her foot for her shoe. He hadn't realized until now that she had kicked them off when she sat down. It made what had happened even more intimate somehow, if that was possible. She kept her eyes on him the entire time. ''You look like you're fleeing.''

He didn't like the accusation, especially since it had a grain of truth in it. Shea raised his head, annoyed. ''I don't run.''

''Good.'' She gestured to the place he had vacated. ''Do you want to sit and talk?''

''No.'' He shifted uncomfortably, then damned her for doing this to him. Most of all, he damned himself for letting it happen. And for feeling.

''Why?''

Shea turned away and looked toward the door. He had to leave. ''There's nothing to talk about.''

She reached for his hand, forcing him to look at her. ''I think there is.''

He knew she wouldn't stop until he gave her some sort of an answer. He settled for part of the truth. "You're a very attractive woman."

Dottie inclined her head. "Thank you."

"And I'm a man."

"I noticed."

She was making this difficult on purpose, he thought. "And your dress doesn't quite cling to you whenever you exhale."

She took a moment before answering. "And that's it?"

He knew it was brutal, but it was better to hurt her now than somehow hurt her later. "That's it." Shea squared his shoulders. "In my old neighborhood, that was enough."

His words stung, but she didn't believe he meant them. He was afraid of something. What, she didn't know. But she intended to. "But you moved out of your neighborhood a long time ago."

He shrugged. "Old habits die hard."

"If you say so," she answered primly, suppressing a smile. She wasn't convinced. Not at all. That hadn't been a casual kiss, or a kiss for merely ending an evening. There had been something more. A lot more. She couldn't shake the feeling that he was running from something, no matter what he said to the contrary.

"I say so."

Dottie rose to her feet. "All right, for now, we'll have it your way."

He looked at her suspiciously. "What do you mean, for now?"

Her smile told him nothing. Except, perhaps, to beware. "Just what I said. Tomorrow's Sunday, and—"

"I have an auction to go to," he said quickly, giving himself an excuse not to go along on another outing. The last thing he needed was to spend more time with her. In order to induce a cure, one had to be away from the source of the infection.

"An auction?"

"Antiques, you know—" he couldn't help himself "—the things that have aliases. They're having an antique auction in Los Angeles and I—"

"I was just about to say that I was going to give Al the day off." She smiled at him, pleased with the way things were turning out. "I'll be free all day." She thought of Mama Marino's weekly Sunday dinner. Mama would understand if she begged off this time. Maybe. Especially if she explained. Mama had been saving her wedding gown for her for a long time and started talking about making alterations on it each time Dottie dated someone more than once. "I've never been to an auction."

"And you'd like to go," he guessed.

"Yes."

He couldn't help smiling. "Don't beat around the bush much, do you?"

"What would be the point?" she asked innocently.

Survival, for one, he thought. His. "I thought you didn't like antiques."

"I'm always open to a good argument."

Of that he had absolutely no doubt. "What does arguing have to do with it?"

"You could try to convince me about the merits of surrounding yourself with used furniture that costs too much."

He shook his head, marveling. "Pretty outspoken, aren't you?"

"Yes."

Maybe it would be fun at that, sharing the excitement of securing a new piece. "I suppose it's only fair, since you're teaching Al everything else, that I teach you a little about antiques."

She linked her arm through his as they walked to her front door. Out of the corner of his eye, he saw the pig shuffle into the dining room. When he turned to mention the fact to Dottie, he saw that she was shaking her head at the pig. Howard retreated. The woman was one of a kind, all right.

"You believe in fair play?" Dottie asked, picking up on the word he had used.

"Yes."

"So do I." Her eyes danced as she smiled at him. "Most of the time."

Wicked, Shea thought. There was something wicked about her smile even as it was innocent. Why did he feel as if he had been put on notice?

"All right, if you really want to attend. The auction is at three. I'll pick you up here at two."

She nodded. "I'll be ready."

He turned to leave, then thought it best to say one more thing. "And Dottie?"

She watched his mouth as he spoke, reliving the way it had felt against hers. "Yes?"

He took one last, lingering look at her dress. With his hand on the door, he felt that he safely could. "Wear something—" He searched for the right word. None quite covered it. He settled on "Warmer."

She grinned at the properness of his words, wondering how long it would take to peel away the layers and find the basic man beneath, the man who had risen up from the streets. "As in generating heat or preserving it?"

One brow arched in amusement despite himself. "As in clothing. A lot of it."

She tilted her head back, her long, straight hair gliding along the planes of her shoulders, and laughed. "That isn't going to protect you, you know."

The laugh died a little as she looked at him. The corners of her mouth were still lifted in a smile, but there was a seriousness to it that he could not miss. "Or me."

"No," he was forced to agree. "But it's a start."

And there would be no finish, he thought as he closed the door behind him and walked to his car.

Chapter Six

Being twenty-seven years old with a degree in child psychology didn't really help. It didn't change a thing.

Dottie sighed. She reached for the phone several times before actually lifting the receiver from the cradle. She held her hand poised over the buttons. There would be no recriminations, no harsh words. Just quiet acceptance. Very quiet acceptance. The guilt would be awful. As a psychologist, she could understand all aspects of the situation, her feelings, her mother's feelings, the reasons behind them. But it didn't make any of it easier.

As she tapped out the familiar numbers, she was fourteen again, standing in Mama's kitchen, about to make some confession Mama wasn't going to like.

Waldo leaped up on the sofa and curled up at her feet, as if he understood that she needed moral support. Dottie leaned forward and petted the shaggy head. A pink tongue licked her ankles.

A warm, heavily accented voice answered on the third ring. The telephone was in the kitchen and Mama was almost always in the kitchen, especially today, since it was Sunday. But she didn't move with the same agility that she used to.

"Hallo?"

"Mama, it's Dottie." She steeled herself for what she knew was to come. "I'm afraid that I won't be able to make lunch today."

"Oh?"

It was only one word, but it could send guilt hurtling through a brick wall at thirty paces. In Mama's hands, creating feelings of guilt where once there were none had developed into an art form. She used her talent to cut away any lies, which she euphemistically called "false excuses."

Sundays were precious to Bridgette Marino. She liked to see her family gather around the long, spacious dining room table that Papa had made for her as a wedding present, promising to one day fill all the chairs. When they couldn't have any more children after Angelo, they had opened their hearts to Dottie and her brother.

And all, Mama said, she asked in return was an hour, "or maybe two," on Sunday. To tempt, she prepared her meals accordingly. Each and every Sunday, everyone's favorite dish made some sort of token appearance on her table to insure that everyone was happy and everyone ate.

To help stem the tide of the ocean of guilt Mama sent her way, Dottie said, "I have a date, Mama."

Although there was still silence, it was of a different sort. It was no longer the silence of disappointment, of hurt feelings, but the silence of mulling over a good piece of news. "Bring him."

Dottie knew she'd say that. "Can't. He's taking me to an auction."

Mama paused, thinking. "We could move dinner. Later. Earlier."

Have stove, will travel, Dottie thought. "No, not on my account."

"Then on whose?" Mama demanded as if Dottie had just said something stupid. "I am not the one with a date." The older woman's voice softened. "If I do not make the adjustments, then who will? Family is all there is, Dorothea."

And she was hers, Dottie thought affectionately, if not in blood, then in spirit. Never once had the woman ever treated Angelo any differently than she had treated Shad and herself, even though Angelo had been nurtured in her womb.

Dottie pulled her feet back from Waldo, who had suddenly decided to declare them fair game. She shook her head and pointed to the floor. Waldo jumped off.

"I know, Mama, but I'm not sure when the auction will be over and—" She didn't want Mama to pounce on Shea just yet. She didn't think he was prepared to weather that sort of a thing so soon.

Mama cut to the heart of the matter. "How well do you know him?"

Ah, here it came, the friendly inquisition. "Just a week."

"And how do you feel about him?"

Mama always wanted things done yesterday and everything in its place today. Just like her, she smiled to herself, getting a taste of her own medicine. "Mama, he's only kissed me once."

"Once is enough if it is the right man. When your Papa kissed me," she began in her easy manner, her voice growing softer as she remembered. Never, in all the time Dottie could remember, did Mama ever refer to Salvatore as her foster father. He was always "Papa." And she was Mama from the moment they had first walked in through the Marinos' front door all those years ago. "It was in the spring, in Milano. I was sixteen. No experience," she added needlessly. "But I knew. I knew he was the only one for me."

There was an expectant silence. She knew her children very well, Dottie thought.

"Maybe," Dottie finally said.

"Maybe?" The word was drawn out. Dottie could tell Mama didn't believe her vague answer. And suspected a good deal more.

Dottie hedged, something she wasn't very good at. "There are answers I need first, Mama."

"We all need answers, Dorothea," Mama said wisely. "But they do not come all at once." Dottie could hear the broad smile in her voice. Bridgette Marino must have been a lusty woman in her time. "That is part of the fun."

"I'll remember that." Dottie laughed.

"So," the woman tried one last time. "Your place will be empty today?"

Dottie tucked the twinge of guilt away. It wasn't the end of the world if she didn't come. She knew that. Yet she found herself wanting to be in two places at the same time. And wanting Shea to meet this remarkable woman. "I'm afraid so."

Mama sighed dramatically. "Have a good time."

"I will," she promised.

"And see if he has a sister for Angelo."

She never stopped. "Mama, Angelo will find a woman in his own good time."

"Yes, I am sure. But I would like to be alive to see it."

Dottie shook her head as she rose from the sofa. "I love you, Mama." In the background, she heard the clang of a pot. If she closed her eyes, Dottie could see the woman bustling around the country kitchen, plumes of steam rising from all the cast iron pots on the stove as enticing aromas flooded the four corners of the kitchen and wafted into the rest of the house.

"But of course." Dottie heard a spoon rattle as Mama set it down on the counter. "I love you, too. This man taking you to the action—"

"Auction," Dottie corrected.

"Auction," Mama repeated. "The one who kissed you, he has a name?"

Relentless, that was Mama. "Shea Delany."

"Tell this Shea Delany hello for me and that I would like to see him at my table. Soon."

"Yes, Mama." She placed the telephone on the table. "Ciao."

"Ciao."

Mama always made everything sound so simple, Dottie thought. That's why she always liked talking to her. Mama had a way of burrowing through all the obstacles, cutting them away and laying siege to the heart of the matter. She would brook no nonsense, but gave back oceans of love in return.

Slightly overbearing or not, Shea would like her, she decided. Everyone liked Mama. She'd find a way to bring him to dinner, just as Mama "requested." She'd just have to tell Mama to hold the orange blossoms and not toss them at Shea as he walked through the door.

Dottie grinned as she walked out of the living room, Waldo hurrying close behind. Dinner would have to be engineered very carefully. But she had a feeling that a dose of family closeness would be good for Shea. As well as for Al.

She was getting ahead of herself. As usual.

Dottie walked into her room and crossed to the closet. "Okay, what does one wear to an auction?"

Waldo barked a suggestion.

* * *

Basically, he was a loner. Other than enjoying the company of his daughter, Shea liked doing things alone. He preferred his own company, his own counsel, to that of others. Years ago, when he was young and there was only the thought of today, not tomorrow, he had enjoyed rousing, noisy parties and companions whose only quest in life was to have a good time.

Shea had had his thrills, run with the wrong crowd and almost seen his own end stare him in the face by the age of seventeen. He'd had enough of the wild life, enough of life filled with people he neither really knew nor wanted to know.

Now, as his own man, he liked to do things by himself. He ran his business that way, trusting a few key people. But only so far. At any given moment, he knew the inventory of each of his stores, was familiar with the work record of each of his employees. He was proud of the fact that he was always on top of things.

But always, always alone. After Sandra died, there was no reason to be otherwise.

So why was he taking this woman, his daughter's *tutor* to an auction? This wasn't an afternoon of pleasure he was facing. He was working, securing pieces for his various clients. Julius, his head assistant at the Beverly Hills store, went to auctions, but only when Shea was otherwise occupied. The responsibility was predominantly his. If Julius went, he went with a list drawn up by Shea. Shea believed in controlling everything. That way, nothing controlled him.

How was he supposed to think with a talkative blonde sitting next to him?

This was, Shea decided as he brought his car up to her driveway and turned off the engine, a very bad idea. How was he going to get out of it? And why the hell had he invited her along in the first place?

He hadn't, he remembered as he got out of the car and slammed the door shut behind him. She had invited herself. Shea ran his hand through his hair. Well, he would just have to uninvite her.

With that resolved, Shea rang the doorbell and heard a chorus of dogs barking. He was surprised that the pig wasn't braying or howling or whatever it was that Vietnamese pot belly pigs did.

Dottie opened the door just as he was about to ring again. Shea began to tell her that there had been a change in plans and he was going to have to go to the auction by himself.

At least, that was what he was prepared to say. That was what he thought he was *going* to say. He got as far as opening his mouth and then he made the mistake of looking at her.

She was wearing red. A red two-piece suit, cinched at the waist with a short skirt that flared slightly. Lace peeked out from the cuffs and foamed seductively at her throat. Her hair was piled high in something resembling a Gibson-girl hairstyle. Soft wisps whispered against her neck, teasingly begging him to press his lips against it.

Shea lost his train of thought.

For his benefit, she pivoted slowly in a complete circle. "Conservative enough?" she asked as she turned to face him.

He was tempted to pull out a few pins and watch her hair tumble down like blond water, then run his fingers through it, savoring the texture. "What makes you think you had to dress conservatively?"

"I didn't want to stand out."

As if anything could negate that. Shea shook his head. "Then I suggest you wear a gunnysack. Over your entire body. Starting with your face."

He was going to have to do something about this, about his reactions every time he was near Dottie. And soon. He had a feeling that things were going to get out of control if he didn't.

Dottie raised one eyebrow. "Was that a compliment, Mr. Delany?"

"I guess it was." He looked over her shoulder, hoping to change the subject. "Where are all your little friends? I heard them making noise when I rang."

"They're around." She nodded behind her. "Would you like to come in for a while?"

No, that would definitely be a mistake. He remembered last night. If he didn't want things going any farther between them, he definitely couldn't risk situations where he'd be alone with her.

The idea made him smile slightly. Shea Delany, running from an encounter with a beautiful woman. Who would have thought the day would ever come? But then, who would have ever thought that Shea Delany would develop a conscience? Or live to get out of the neighborhood and become a success?

He glanced at his watch. "No, I think we should get going."

She had seen interest flare in his eyes for a moment before they had gone flat. He wanted to come inside. What made him hesitate and then refuse? "Fine. I'll get my purse."

The auction attracted an elite, highly polished class of people. He scarcely had to glance around to know that she was the most beautiful one here. A sparkling ruby in an old setting.

She absorbed it all with interest, the scores of tastefully dressed people milling about, talking in hushed tones, perusing their catalogs and hastily penciling in things at whim. "Are these all dealers?" She had never given antique collecting much thought before Shea had entered her life.

He liked the way curiosity seemed to heighten her features, making her eyes larger. And he enjoyed the fact that she was asking him about something he could readily and easily discuss. This wasn't private. There was no pain here. Though antiques were not his passion, the way they had been for Mr. Flanders, the man responsible for first introducing him to this world, they were certainly his pleasure.

"Dealers and private collectors." He accepted a catalog with the items for auction from one of the hostesses, then took one for Dottie as well. "They all come out for one of these to try to make a killing or to fill their inventory." He handed her the catalog. "Or just because they've heard that a particular piece is up for bid."

Dottie flipped through a few pages in the catalog. All the items were numbered and glowingly described. "Do you know what you're bidding on, or are you going to wait until the spirit moves you when you see something?"

That would be the way she would proceed, he thought. When something moved her. Once, that would have been his way, too. But he had long since buried that impetuous youth whose past had been marked for oblivion.

Shea tapped his pamphlet absently, or maybe to still the nerves he felt tightening. "I've already gone through the catalog very thoroughly. Impulse is something I no longer act on."

Oh, I don't know about that, Dottie thought, not bothering to suppress her smile.

He saw the look in her sea green eyes as she turned toward him. Instinctively, he knew that she was thinking about last night. Well, why shouldn't she? He had been thinking about nothing else himself, even though he had tried to block it from his mind. It seemed absolutely incredible to him that after all his experience with women, this one woman would linger in his thoughts like a haunting melody that refused to fade.

And all he had done was kiss her.

"Sometimes impulses are good." She looked to her left and saw that there was another room off to the side with a guard standing in the doorway. Was that where everything was kept?

"And sometimes they're not," Shea answered firmly. Like last night's. All that had done was to remind him, to stir him. To torture him with what he couldn't allow himself to have. The excitement he had felt last night went well beyond mere physical attraction. It was an indiscernible feeling. He couldn't say that it was similar to what he had experienced with his wife. But it had brought back memories.

The textbooks she had so neatly stacked in her office would say that he was into denial. But she wasn't thinking clinically right now. Mama was right, she decided, sometimes all it took was one kiss to crystallize things. Dottie made up her mind that this man was going to be part of her life for a long, long time.

The trick, it seemed, was to get him to consciously want to be there.

He saw her looking off to the left. "Some of the pieces are still on display before the auction begins. Would you like to view them?"

She was already moving in that direction. "That's why I'm here."

No, he thought, taking her arm as they circumvented three stern-looking men he recognized as local competitors. *You're here to haunt me. To act as my own personal purgatory. And for some unknown damn reason, I seem to be trying to help you do exactly that.*

There were a total of three guards in the other room. One at each entrance and one just milling around. But not aimlessly. One look at his eyes told Dottie that. The man was alert and watching. Within the room were rows of long, linen-covered tables displaying some of the smaller pieces that would be put up for auction.

The auction was called the Saunders Collection. It was hard to believe that all this had been in the possession of one individual. "All this belonged to one man?" she asked aloud in amazement.

"Yes." Shea wondered if she knew how seductive she looked with surprise widening her features. He had to keep telling himself that this was not the place to explore these feelings. No place was.

It was on the tip of her tongue to ask why anyone would want to surround himself with things like this, but everyone had his passion.

What was Shea's?

She knew he truly liked antiques, but it wasn't the same as having a passion for them. Passion was something that lit a flame in your heart and showed in your eyes. There was only admiration and interest in his eyes when he looked at the pieces before them.

But there had been passion in his eyes for a fleeting moment last night, after he had kissed her. She hadn't been mistaken about that, no matter how cool and collected he tried to be today.

Taking Dottie by the arm, he directed her toward several pieces he thought might be of mild interest to her. He could understand her initial feelings. When Mr. Flanders had proudly displayed his collection for him, he had viewed them in the same manner, with the same polite disinterest. It seemed like one of life's ironies that ultimately antiques had proven to be his way off the streets in a neighborhood where stereotypically you either shot your way out or were shot. Antiques and guts. And a willingness to do whatever it took to get out. On the right side of the law. He had been on the wrong side and knew there was nothing there but a dead end.

"You don't like antiques," he observed, amused, "do you?"

She hadn't realized that she was being obvious about it. "It's not that I don't like them, it's just that they're—" She searched for a good word to describe her feelings and found none. "Old," she finally said for lack of a better term.

The man next to her gave Dottie an annoyed look as he overheard her comment. Shea's amusement grew. She was voicing sentiments that he had once harbored. Before he learned. "That's what makes them antiques."

"Old reminds me of poverty." She remembered Mama's deep pleasure in finally getting a new piece of furniture as Papa's business took a turn for the better. "Of not being able to afford new things. Of 'making do.'" She searched his eyes, wondering if he understood and found herself floating in them instead. He had beautiful liquid eyes that could hold her soul captive.

Shea laughed. "Have you seen the price tags on some of these 'old' things?" He gestured at a table with several pieces of old jewelry on it.

Dottie raised her hands. "I know, I know. Still, it's an emotional thing," she admitted easily, "not a logical thing."

"Interesting sentiment for a psychologist to have." He drew her over to another table.

Dottie grinned at his comment. "I never said I was orthodox."

"No, that you did not."

She looked around, but couldn't find any furniture in the room beyond the tables and several folding chairs. "Is what you're planning to bid on here?"

"Some of it."

"Show me." Easily, Dottie linked her fingers through his.

It seemed so natural, he almost forgot that a week ago, he hadn't known her at all. He led her to the last row in the back and pointed out a small box, barely twelve inches wide. "This is the one."

She had to admit that it didn't really impress her. "I thought you only dealt in furniture."

"The Beverly Hills store is branching out. Eventually, all of them will. I'm starting small."

She looked back at the box. The catalog listed it as item fifty-three, a lady's dressing case, Victorian brass bound and inlaid with rosewood. "Yes, that's small all right. How old is it?"

"It was made around 1863."

She reached out to touch it without thinking and he quickly placed his hand over hers. The momentary warm contact was all that was necessary to bring back last night. Shea removed his hand.

"I think the guard is having a heart attack." He nodded toward his left. He didn't bother to add that his was not in the greatest condition either. Shea thought it ridiculous for a man his age to react this way.

She flashed a smile at the short, gray-uniformed man. "Sorry, habit," she told Shea. "I tend to want to touch things."

Yes, he'd noticed. "Then you like it?"

"No," she answered honestly. "But it's a piece of history. Some man gave this to his bride on their wedding night."

"How did you know that?" He didn't remember reading that in the catalog. He flipped it open to scan the section.

"I don't. But it's the kind of thing a man would do back then. Wonderfully romantic, don't you think?"

"Wonderfully creative is more like it."

She laughed. "Life would be very dull without embellishments."

"I find life exciting enough just the way it is." He looked at the back of her head as she turned around. *Maybe a little too much so,* he added silently.

"Oh, how lovely." She looked down at a brooch that was propped up at the end of the display.

He caught the warm note in her voice. "Do you like it?"

"A woman can always appreciate fine jewelry," she answered with a smile. She held her hands up. "See, no touching."

He took one of her hands in his, guided by instincts that were far older than he.

"Ladies and gentlemen." They turned to see a tall man standing in the doorway that connected the two rooms. The man clasped his long, slender hands together, waiting for complete attention to turn his way. When there was silence, he continued. "The auction is about to begin. If everyone will please be seated?"

Shea moved to leave. Dottie turned around and took one last look at the cameo, then let him lead her out of the room. "You know, this *is* kind of exciting."

"Looking at antiques?" He wouldn't have thought that she'd be the type to pander to what she felt were his interests. She struck him as too much of her own person for that.

"No, bidding. Winning."

That, he thought as they took seats near the front in the large room, was more in keeping with her personality. And that was something he could understand. His adrenaline always flowed when bidding began. It was a holdover from his early years when the roll of the dice or the turn of a card could mean the difference between eating and not eating. The anticipation of winning hummed through his blood.

It was something akin, he suddenly realized, to what he experienced when he had kissed her.

In the background, he heard a gavel being struck. It was time to turn his attention to the reason he was here. But with Dottie sitting next to him, he knew it wasn't going to be easy.

The more
you love romance . . .
the more
you'll love this offer

FREE!

Mail this
heart today!
(See inside)

Join us on a Silhouette® Honeymoon
and we'll give you
4 Free Books
A Free Victorian Picture Frame
And a Free Mystery Gift

IT'S A
SILHOUETTE HONEYMOON—
A SWEETHEART OF A FREE OFFER!
HERE'S WHAT YOU GET:

1. Four New Silhouette Romance™ Novels—FREE!

Take a Silhouette Honeymoon with your four exciting romances—yours FREE from the Silhouette Reader Service™. Each of these hot-off-the-press novels brings you the passion and tenderness of today's greatest love stories...your free passports to bright new worlds of love and foreign adventure.

2. Lovely Victorian Picture Frame—FREE!

This lovely Victorian pewter-finish miniature is perfect for displaying a treasured photograph. And it's yours FREE as added thanks for giving our Reader Service a try!

3. An Exciting Mystery Bonus—FREE!

You'll be thrilled with this surprise gift. It is useful as well as practical.

4. Free Home Delivery!

Join the Silhouette Reader Service™ and enjoy the convenience of previewing 6 new books every month delivered right to your home. Each book is yours for only $2.25* each, a saving of 34¢ each off the cover price per book—and there is no extra charge for postage and handling. It's a sweetheart of a deal for you! If you're not completely satisfied, you may cancel at any time, for any reason, simply by sending us a note or shipping statement marked "cancel" or by returning any shipment to us at our cost.

5. Free Newsletter!

You'll get our monthly newsletter, packed with news about your favorite writers, upcoming books, even recipes from your favorite authors.

6. More Surprise Gifts!

Because our home subscribers are our most valued readers, when you join the Silhouette Reader Service™, we'll be sending you additional free gifts from time to time—as a token of our appreciation.

START YOUR SILHOUETTE HONEYMOON TODAY—
JUST COMPLETE, DETACH AND MAIL YOUR FREE-OFFER CARD

*Terms and prices subject to change without notice. Sales tax applicable in NY. Offer limited to one per household and not valid to current Silhouette Romance™ subscribers. All orders subject to approval.

START YOUR
SILHOUETTE HONEYMOON TODAY.
JUST COMPLETE, DETACH AND MAIL YOUR
FREE-OFFER CARD.

If offer card below is missing write to:
Silhouette Reader Service, 3010 Walden Ave.,
P.O. Box 1867, Buffalo, NY 14269-1867.

DETACH AND MAIL TODAY!

BUSINESS REPLY MAIL
FIRST CLASS MAIL   PERMIT NO. 717   BUFFALO, NY

POSTAGE WILL BE PAID BY ADDRESSEE

SILHOUETTE READER SERVICE
3010 WALDEN AVE
PO BOX 1867
BUFFALO NY 14240-9952

NO POSTAGE
NECESSARY
IF MAILED
IN THE
UNITED STATES

Chapter Seven

"Are you sure this is an auction?" Dottie whispered, leaning toward Shea.

The feel of her breath along his cheek, sweet and warm and enticingly seductive, distracted him for a moment. "Yes, why?"

She nodded toward the tall, well-dressed angular man standing behind the podium. "The auctioneer isn't talking fast. I can understand every word he's saying." She had envisioned rapid-fire words that would make her head spin. This was rather subdued.

Shea laughed softly as he inclined his head toward her. He caught the fragrance of her shampoo, something clean, yet sexy. "That's the idea."

It still didn't seem right to her. Auctions should generate electricity, excitement. The bald, aristocratic man with the gavel might as well have been ordering tea in an exclusive restaurant for all the emotion he was displaying. "I guess having to deal with a lot of money tends to slow you down."

Shea gave her a pointed, knowing look. He sensed she was challenging him, intimating that he was slow to warm to her. A lot she knew. "Not necessarily."

She caught the look in his eye and felt a shiver of anticipation sliding down her back and unsettling the pit of her stomach. "Nice to know." Dottie didn't bother to try to hide her smile as she looked down at the catalog in her lap.

The auction had been going on for an hour and Shea still hadn't made a single bid. Dottie was beginning to wonder if perhaps this was his idea of an entertaining Sunday afternoon. As she was about to ask, Shea leaned slightly forward. An almost infinitesimal tension entered his body, but she detected it. The warrior girding up for battle. Dottie looked up toward the stage and saw the window seat two attendants were carrying. They placed it next to the podium.

"That?" she asked. It looked ugly to her. Old and ugly. But then, she mused, it *was* an antique.

"That."

Dottie shook her head as she glanced back at her catalog, looking for a description of the piece. "To each his own."

But he didn't hear. It was time for business. This was, without a doubt, the part he enjoyed the most. The challenge of winning. Bidding began at a sum Dottie found incomprehensible.

It continued to escalate.

She leaned back and watched Shea in action. He was cool, but it wasn't difficult for her to see the excitement he was experiencing. It was in his eyes, in the way he leaned slightly forward. In the way he tightened his hand on his catalog.

Bidding lasted five minutes, proceeding like an orderly, exceptionally polite game of tennis, with the ball being lobbed back and forth between four bidders. Suddenly caught up in it, Dottie turned her head, trying to pick out the bidders in the sea of faces. She could only make out one to her far right.

And then one bidder dropped out, the bidding too rich for him. Then two. Then the third. The Regency mahogany window seat was Shea's.

Dottie was momentarily speechless as the amount of Shea's final bid sank in. "Thirteen thousand?" She stared at him incredulously. "Dollars?" She was sophisticated enough to appreciate all art forms and down-to-earth enough to be appalled by that kind of money being spent on a piece of furniture.

"I was prepared to go higher." Shea reached into his jacket pocket to take out one of his business cards. The usher would be by soon to pick it up in order to tag his acquisition.

Dottie felt her mouth go dry. "For a *window seat?*" She couldn't help the squeak in her voice.

"Not just any window seat," he pointed out, his eyes teasing her. "One with a scrolling x-frame that was applied with paterae and joined by spirally reeded arms and stretchers." He couldn't help grinning at the look of amazement on her face. There was a time that he had felt the same way.

"Oh, reeded arms and stretchers." She spread her arms. "Well, that makes all the difference in the world." The woman in front of her turned and gave her an annoyed look. She had let her voice rise again, Dottie realized.

"It does. I have several clients interested in purchasing that sort of piece."

A gangly youth in a suit that was just a little too small for him came up to their row. He leaned over the man to Shea's right, his hand outstretched. Shea casually dropped the business card into it and nodded.

"Still doesn't appeal to you, does it?" Shea asked Dottie.

"No," she whispered, mindful of the woman in front of her.

It didn't appeal to her, but he did. Especially when he grinned like that at her. There was something infinitely appealing and roguish about that grin. It heated her blood and made delicious, wild fantasies take flight in her head. She wished she had known him before the sadness had entered his eyes and before the hard lines had been etched around his mouth. Or had they always been there? Had they been stamped on his face during his struggle to make something of himself, or afterward?

"At least you're honest."

"Always. Occupational habit." Dottie turned her catalog to the next number, doggedly trying to keep tabs on the proceedings. She flipped to the last page then back to her place. Only thirty more items to go. At this rate, they were going to be here at least another hour.

He watched her, the way her hair fell into her eyes as she studied the catalog. He'd been so impressed with what she was doing for Al, he'd almost forgotten how very young she looked. "I thought psychologists were supposed to be intentionally vague and lead patients to their own conclusions."

Dottie brushed her hair aside as she glanced toward the stage. They had cleared away his window seat. "You're not a patient. And I probably couldn't lead you anywhere."

"Don't be so sure of that."

She looked at him in surprise, but Shea had already turned his attention to the next item up for bid.

"And now," the auctioneer proudly announced in his deep, refined voice that didn't begin to match his thin face, "we come to the next item, ladies and gentlemen. A good cameo brooch carved with the bust of a young woman, mounted in a gold frame.''

Dottie recognized it as the piece she had admired in the other room. She would have loved to bid on it herself, but even the beginning bid would probably be far more than she could indulge herself with.

"Shall we begin the bidding at five hundred?" The auctioneer looked around the large hall slowly. "Who'll give me five hundred?"

Not me, Dottie thought.

Shea raised his catalog and the auctioneer nodded toward him.

She looked at Shea in mild surprise. "Jewelry?" She thought he was only interested in furniture and a few knickknacks. Knickknacks that ran into hundreds or thousands of dollars.

"There's always a market for good jewelry." He shrugged casually. She had absolutely no idea why that made her heart skip. It was ridiculous to suppose that he was bidding on the piece because she had told him that she liked it.

But that was exactly what she was thinking.

"I have six-fifty from the gentleman in the back." The auctioneer pointed his gavel toward the far left end of the hall.

She turned slightly and saw a man standing in the back dropping his hand. Shea raised his catalog again, catching the auctioneer's attention. "Seven."

"How much do you plan to bid on it?" Dottie whispered.

He didn't look at her. He couldn't afford to break his concentration. "Whatever it takes."

And then she saw it. It was in his eyes, in his voice. The man who had evolved out of the boy who had made his life on the streets. The one used to taking risks and living on the

edge. Excitement pulsated through her as the bidding rico-
cheted back and forth between Shea and the man in the back
until finally, for the sum of two thousand-five, the brooch
was Shea's.

"You did it!" Carried away with the spirit of the moment, Dottie threw her arms around his neck and kissed
him. It was meant to land on his cheek, but he turned his
face at the last second and their lips met. For one fleeting
moment only.

One moment was long enough to remind. Long enough
to rekindle.

Dottie let her arms slip from around his neck. She took a
deep breath as she looked around, flustered, her blood
pounding in her temples. "Sorry, auctions always make me
breathless and excited."

"I thought you said this was your first." Shea took out
another business card. This time, the usher appeared almost immediately to retrieve it.

Dottie flashed a quick, guileless grin. "It is."

Shea could only shake his head in amusement. She
brought a fresh blush to auctions. To everything in his life,
he realized. Cobwebs had a way of breaking away in her
presence. That could be a dangerous sign, if he was looking
for signs. But he wasn't.

"Dinner?"

Shea slipped his arm through Dottie's as they left the
nearly empty hall. Behind him was an officious-looking
clerk who was filing away a check from Shea as well as the
addresses of the stores where the various pieces were to be
shipped.

"I'd love it." The late afternoon sun felt warm on her face
as they stepped outside the hotel. "I had to skip Mama
Marino's weekly dinner to come along."

He was about to remind her that this was her idea, then thought better of it. He handed his ticket to the parking valet and waited with her under the green awning.

"Mama Marino. That's your stepmother?" He couldn't see any other reason for Dottie to refer to the woman by her surname.

"No, my foster mother."

"Foster mother." He said the words almost mechanically. She had foster parents? He had pictured her in the bosom of a happy, well-to-do family. This changed things considerably. And made him wonder about her attitude. "Then you're an—" He stopped, not wanting to inadvertently tread on any old wounds.

"An orphan?" she supplied easily. The valet held the car door open for her and she got into the passenger side. She waited until Shea was seated next to her. "Probably. My father left when I was an infant. And I really don't remember my mother. Only Shad."

Shea carefully guided the car into the flow of traffic. The restaurant he had in mind wasn't that far away. He glanced at Dottie. How could she be so cheerful, so well adjusted? She had been an orphan. Weren't there any scars over being abandoned?

"Shad's your brother?"

"Yes." Her expression warmed as she thought of Shad, of all the years he had been there for her, grumbling, bullying, loving. "He took care of me when we were at the orphanage. He wouldn't let them separate us when they placed us in foster homes."

"Homes," he repeated. "Then there was more than one?" He couldn't picture this bubbly, confident woman being shunted from one place to another, not even as a young child.

Basically, Dottie had pushed that part of her life from her mind. It was better not to remember. It hadn't been the best of times. She recalled one woman who liked to twist her ear when she didn't mind fast enough. And brush her hair until she cried. They had run away from there, Shad and her, but the lady from the orphanage found them and brought them back.

But it had only been for a short while, until another home was available. The Marinos'. "Yes."

He saw the slight frown and wondered at it. "When did you come to live with the Marinos?"

"When I was six." That was when her life had really started. When she was six. All that came before resided in the past, in a life that had happened to someone else. It was the only way she could bear it. "They've been the only parents I've ever known, really. Papa died a few years ago." Saying it still constricted her throat and made tears form instantly. She had loved him a great deal. Dottie blinked the tears away. "He left his construction business to Angelo and Shad."

Shea turned down the next block and parked the car in the small lot located directly behind the restaurant. "Angelo was his—"

"Is. Angelo very much *is*." She grinned, thinking of him and his funny, warm approach to everything. "He's Papa's natural son. Except that Papa never let us feel that it really made a difference." She took Shea's hand as he offered it to her and slid out of the passenger seat. Appreciating the quick flash of leg as her skirt climbed up her thigh, then fell, he closed the door behind her.

"Mama would like to meet you sometime," she informed him as he escorted her to the restaurant's entrance.

He waited until she had stepped through the doorway. "Why? Two, please, Giles," he said to the heavyset man behind the desk.

The man was dressed, Dottie realized, like the owner of an inn. An inn built in the seventeen-hundreds. Right down to his silver buckled shoes and the small pigtail at his nape.

"This way, please, Mr. Delany." The man led the way down a single step into a pleasantly lit dining room with early American tables and benches. Dottie glanced over her shoulder at Shea. She might have known he'd bring her to a place like this. She felt as if she had stepped through a time portal into the past.

Dottie slipped into the booth, then answered Shea's question. "Mama likes to take an interest in my life and the people I meet."

Shea sat across from Dottie and accepted the menus the host handed them. "Are you planning to bring all your patients to her as well?"

"Only when she makes lasagna." She noticed that the host had a wistful look on his face as he moved away. She glanced at the menu and realized why. There was only one item listed on the menu under main course. The description went on for a quarter of a page.

"They specialize in prime rib," Shea explained in answer to the mild look of surprise on her face. "You do like prime rib, don't you?" It was a little late to ask, but he had just assumed she did. And he really had wanted to bring her here.

"I love it." She closed her menu and looked around. The room was completely filled, as was, from what she could see, the room just beyond. The lighting was dim, coming from hurricane lamps hung in various locations. The decor was early American. There was even a musket and powder horn hung above the archway between the two dining rooms. All the waitresses were dressed as serving wenches and the tableware appeared to be pewter. "I can see why you like this place."

"Actually, I helped them get their furnishings at a rather good price. In exchange," he unfolded his napkin, "they promised to always be able to seat me whenever I came for dinner."

She looked around. They *did* have the last booth. "Even if there are no tables?"

He smiled at her. "This is the owner's private booth. He reserves it for family and friends." He liked being able to say that. It was important to him that she knew he was liked. Because he wanted her to like him.

A waitress, her blond hair trying vainly to slip out from beneath her cap, presented a bottle of cider wine to Shea. "Giles just told me you were here. Compliments of the house, Mr. Delany." She placed the bottle and two glasses on the table, gave Shea what Dottie took for rather an intimate smile and slowly turned her attention to the next booth.

Dottie watched as Shea poured her a glass. "Everyone know your name here?"

"That's Cynthia." He filled his own glass, then set the bottle down. "She's the owner's daughter."

"Oh." Dottie looked at Cynthia as she wrote down the next table's order for dessert. The woman's blouse was off her shoulders, edged in flowing lace and revealed more than a little cleavage. "She's very healthy looking. Must come from carrying all those trays."

Shea hid his amusement and tapped the menu. "Would you like an appetizer?"

She glanced at the menu. Mama's dinners were seven-course affairs, but she had little appetite this afternoon. Her stomach had an unaccustomed flutter in it.

"No." She leaned forward, holding her glass so that it caught the light from the overhead lantern. She watched it bounce and shimmer for a moment. "But I would like some information."

Shea took a sip of wine, then placed his glass on the table, still holding the stem. "About?"

Dottie raised her eyes to his face. He looked so rugged, so sensual in this light. She caught herself wishing he'd kiss her again. "You. I've told you about my background."

He leaned back. He didn't enjoy talking about his past. He was only interested in where he was going, not where he had been. There was too much pain buried there. And things he was ashamed of. "I didn't exactly force it out of you."

Dottie went on, undaunted. "Meaning that I'll have to pry it out of you?"

She made him think of that dust mop of hers, clamping down on something and holding on relentlessly. "Is this necessary to help Al?"

"No." She regarded her glass and chose her words carefully. It was like picking out a path through a mine field and she had no idea why. "It's necessary to help me. By the time I've known someone a week, I usually have their complete life story, including what kindergarten they attended."

He looked away. He didn't like being probed. "I didn't 'attend' kindergarten."

"Ah, progress."

The teasing delight in her voice made him laugh. And then he stopped. If he hadn't wanted her to ask, then he wouldn't have taken her out to dinner. He knew by now what she was like. Maybe talking would be all right, just this once.

Shea shrugged as he toyed with his wine, suddenly wishing for something with a kick. Like the tangy, tempting taste of her mouth. "There's nothing much to tell."

The hell there isn't. "You were born in the heart of Hell's Kitchen in New York and you wound up owning and operating five stores that deal in expensive antiques and a clientele that reads like a who's who list of international celebrities." She leaned her chin on the palm of her upturned hand. "Didn't something happen in between?"

She seemed to have done her homework. He wondered why. "You tell me." He turned as Cynthia returned for their order. "Two dinners, Cynthia." Shea looked at Dottie. "You seem to have all the answers."

"No, what I have is an article." She tore off a piece of bread and buttered it lavishly. "An old article, from a newspaper." She took a bite and savored the taste for a moment. She absolutely loved crisp, fresh-baked bread. "By the way," she wiped the corner of her mouth with her napkin, "you should sue the photographer. He didn't begin to do you justice."

A tiny crumb remained just at the edge of her mouth. Shea leaned forward and brushed it away, his thumb lightly skimming her lip. He dropped his hand as he felt another strong shaft of desire pierce through him. He wanted her. Badly. It annoyed him that he couldn't control that. "You always say what you think?"

She saw the look that entered his eyes and then left. She felt her own excitement building. "It saves time." She dragged a breath in. The wine wasn't helping her to maintain a clear head. "Now, are you going to tell me anything, or are we going to make polite, meaningless conversation all evening that neither one of us is interested in? Thank you." She nodded at the waitress as the large pewter plate was set down in front of her.

"Careful," the waitress warned. "It's hot."

It wasn't the only thing, Shea thought. "And if I opt for the latter?" he asked Dottie as soon as the waitress had left.

"You'll be missing something," she told him simply. "Mmm, this is good." The first mouthful all but melted on her tongue.

Though he always enjoyed eating here, the last thing on his mind right now was food. "Which is?"

Dottie stopped, her fork poised over the next piece. "Connecting with another human being."

He watched shifting shadows and lights from the flickering hurricane lamp play on her face, caressing it the way he longed to. Urges shimmered through him. He struggled in vain to deny them. "Maybe I don't want to connect. Maybe remaining at a distance is what I prefer."

He was lying and they both knew it. The smile on her lips said so. "Then you wouldn't have kissed me the way you did last night. Or this afternoon at the auction."

"This afternoon," he pointed out, "you kissed me."

Her grin grew broader as she shook her head. "Picky, picky." Setting the utensils on her plate, she leaned forward over the wooden table. Her eyes were mischievous. "Now are you going to personalize this conversation, or do I have to get nasty?"

He laughed, raising his hands in surrender, though it might have been fun to see what she meant by "nasty." "It wasn't that interesting a life."

She had her doubts about that. "But it was yours and I'd like to hear it." Her voice grew serious as the teasing look left her eyes. "Really."

He could have resisted her words. He couldn't resist the sincerity in her eyes. "My father abandoned us when I was one."

She thought of her own. Not even a face on a faded photograph. "We have something in common."

Shea had no idea why her words warmed him the way they did. "And my mother, well, she did what she could for a while, but then it was easier for her to drink and forget that life hurt." An image came to him of a woman who had misspent her youth and slipped into old age years before she should have. Of a hand raised to strike, not to comfort. Of a dark, lonely room he never liked to be in.

"And you?" That was what she was interested in. How he had survived and come to this.

He shrugged carelessly, wanting to dismiss what never really faded from his mind for long. "I raised myself. Ran numbers as a kid for extra money." His mouth hardened as pieces of memories came and left, uncompleted. "And got tough very, very fast."

She didn't want to dwell on the wounds. "How did you get into antiques?"

He laughed shortly. "Long story." Shea turned his attention to his dinner. It was getting cold.

"I'm not going anywhere. We haven't even had our second glass of wine."

He picked up the bottle and poured them each another glass. "You're determined, aren't you?"

"Absolutely."

Shea took a sip of wine and then ate. She thought that she had lost him when he suddenly said, more to the plate than to her, "It was after I got out of reform school." Shea raised his eyes to her face, waiting for the shock, the revulsion, to set in. If it did, there was no evidence of it in her expression. It remained unchanged. "Doesn't that shock you?"

"Not particularly," she answered matter-of-factly, then gave the matter some thought, "although I wouldn't have chosen antiques to get into."

"I meant about the reform school." She knew damn well what he meant, he thought.

She smiled. There was a trace of sympathy in her eyes, but not the pity that he would have expected. "Not particularly."

"Most people would be."

"I'm not most people." How did she make him understand that? And trust her? "Anyway, you seem to have survived it well enough. What did you do to get sent there?"

The scene came back to him, even though he tried to block it out. The judge who had looked at him as if he was less than human. "The charge was stealing a car."

"The charge," she repeated. He hadn't been guilty of it. She was willing to bet anything on that. "What was the offense?"

She had caught the difference. It surprised him. And pleased him.

"A harmless prank, I thought. Joyriding. I didn't know the car was stolen. My friend told me it was his older brother's car." He thought of the battered, lime green car. "It certainly didn't look worth stealing. So I went along." An ironic smile twisted his lips. "And the police caught us fifteen minutes later. They didn't believe me when I said I had nothing to do with stealing it."

She thought of him, young, frightened, alone. "And there wasn't anyone to take your side?"

He laughed at the thought. "Who was going to take the side of a high school dropout with a bad reputation?" He had begged his mother to come down. But she had been so far withdrawn into her own world by then, she hadn't even understood what he was saying.

Dottie placed her hand over his. "I would have."

He searched her face to see if she was lying. She wasn't. "You believe me?"

"Yes."

"Why?"

She saw the suspicion in his eyes. "Why would you lie to me?"

"Why not?"

It was simple enough to her. "You haven't got anything to gain."

Maybe. Maybe not. But he wanted the subject closed. "Is that enough of a 'personalized' conversation for you?"

"As an appetizer, yes."

"What's the main course?" he asked more gamely than he thought possible.

"You were going to tell me how you got into antiques."

"A work/study program," he answered in a monotone. "They sent me to Jacob Flanders, an old man who needed help distributing his stock to candy stores. He dabbled in antiques on the side. Lived and breathed them in his spare time, actually. He took a liking to me."

"And the rest, as they say—" she grinned, letting him off the hook for a moment "—is history."

"Yes, it is."

As was the rest of his life. And it was going to stay that way.

Chapter Eight

The study of human nature had always fascinated Dottie. Shea Delany intrigued her even more. She let a little time and a little wine pass before she asked her next question. "A candy store seems a long way from an antique shop."

He might have known that she wouldn't be satisfied with half answers. He decided to indulge her a little more. As long as he maintained control over the conversation, it was all right. But there was one area he had no intention of letting her delve into.

"He didn't run a candy store. He supplied them." Shea thought back and the years seemed to melt away. He could see Flanders, hunched over his desk, writing notes, his small, precise handwriting flowing over the pages. "It was nothing more than a dirty little storefront with a battered secondhand metal desk and a chair that fell over if you leaned too far to the right. He kept his inventory inside the basement. Boxes and boxes of little dolls, combs, trinkets that kids liked to spent their money on." He remembered the rundown candy store in his neighborhood. "Or steal."

She felt as if she was intruding on a private memory, but she had to ask. "Did you?"

"From him?" He had been tempted to. In the beginning. But he hadn't. "No. He didn't expect me to. He was the first one who didn't." It had been a new sensation, having someone actually trust him. "So I didn't."

She had wanted to hear him say it.

"Candy stores would call in their orders. So many dozens of this, so many of that. Then I'd go downstairs and fill the order, place it in a cardboard box. We'd fill up the station wagon with all these boxes and twice a week we'd deliver the orders." He remembered it all as if it had taken place yesterday. "Wasn't much, but it provided a living."

"And he liked antiques?"

Shea smiled. "Like" was far from an adequate description. "He had a passion for them. Said they reminded him of his life as a boy in Europe. Mr. Flanders lived in a crammed three-room apartment in Queens, filled to overflowing with things I thought were junk. To him each item was a treasure, treated with reverence and respect. In delivering orders, he traveled through all the little back streets of the city. He found his 'treasures' in old thrift shops. Sometimes on the curb, waiting for the garbage truck. He'd lug them home and restore them."

Shea remembered sweating over an old table one summer. It must have been over a hundred degrees in that old apartment. And they had sat cross-legged on the floor, stripping away an awful coat of bright yellow paint from the table. Together.

"And sold them?" she pressed when he stopped talking. Dottie wondered if he knew that he had loved that old man. It showed in his eyes when he spoke.

Shea shook his head. "And loved them," he corrected. "He kept everything. It got so crowded in the apartment that it was difficult to move around. Yet he refused to part with even one piece." Shea knew how that had to sound. "I guess he was an eccentric in your book."

Did he think she was that judgmental, that shortsighted? "Not necessarily. We all have passions that drive us, that make life interesting. Or if we don't," she added slowly, "we should."

Did she have a passion? Was there something that drove her? "What's yours? Animals?" he guessed, remembering Howard.

She laughed, reading his thoughts. "I like animals, but people are my real passion. I love getting to know people."

Shea placed his spoon on his dish, leaving his dessert half-finished. "Is that what this is all about?"

He knew better than that, she thought. "Yes, in part."

"And what's the other part?" He nodded as the waitress came to clear away his plate.

"I want to get to know about you." Dottie surrendered her own empty plate to the woman. "You make me curious." *And you make my pulse race the way no one's ever done. I want to know everything about you.*

That makes two of us, Shea thought in response. He wanted to get to know everything about her, even though he knew that he shouldn't. He leaned back again. In a way, it felt good remembering, at least this part. This was the part he wasn't ashamed of.

"When he died suddenly, I was eighteen. I came to work one day and he wasn't there. I went to his apartment. He'd given me a key just the week before." Shea ran his tongue over his bottom lip. It was dry. "I found him lying on the floor."

Shea closed his eyes, composing himself as he pushed aside all the grief he had felt at that moment. When he spoke again, his voice was lower, stronger. "He didn't have any family and for some reason, he left everything to me." He looked down at his folded hands, remembering his surprise. "There was a lot more than I thought."

She wanted to reach out, to comfort him. But she could only sit and listen. She knew he wouldn't accept comfort from her. Not yet. "The antiques were worth a lot?"

"That's putting it mildly. But he had saved a lot of money as well. I had never thought of him as well off because he lived so shabbily and his clothes were worn, like mine. I thought he spent all his money restoring his antiques, but I guess he didn't. Even after the large bite the taxes took, there was still enough left over for me to go back to school and then on to college."

"And the antiques?"

"Some of them went to my first store six years later. Most, however," he smiled, "are in my house."

Dottie sipped the last of her coffee. "What made you move from New York to California?"

He had wanted to get as far away from his roots as possible, but he didn't say that. "I had no ties in New York." None he wanted to admit to. His mother had died from an overdose. "Mr. Flanders always said he wanted to go to California. I thought the least I could do was take his furniture there."

It was a sweet gesture. "I didn't picture you as being sentimental."

Shea gave her a sharp look. There were no chinks in his armor. "I'm not."

"No, of course not." Her smile told him that she wasn't buying his denial.

Cynthia came by with the check. Shea placed his credit card on the tray and absently watched her walk away. "I think we've traded enough information for one evening, don't you?"

Because she had been such an attentive audience, he had told her things he had never divulged to anyone else, except Sandra. Sandra had been the same, believing, trusting. Innocent.

And yet, there was something different about this woman. She had a confidence that Sandra hadn't had despite her money, her lineage and her education. Dottie seemed to have come by it the hard way, on her own, just as he had. It gave them something in common.

He didn't want to dwell on what they had in common, or on the way this woman was affecting him, even across the length of the table. He did not commit easily, but when he did, it was with a great intensity. An intensity that had already caused the end of one person's life. He couldn't be responsible for letting something like that happen again. Though he felt extremely drawn to Dottie's enthusiasm, to her zest for life and her optimism, memories of Sandra's death haunted him and kept his emotions behind a impenetrable barrier.

"C'mon." Shea rose and took her arm. "I'd better take you home."

"Will you come in?" Dottie opened the front door and looked at him over her shoulder.

He couldn't say that he wasn't tempted. He was. But he knew that in his present mood, he'd better not give in. Things might happen that he would eventually regret. He'd been knocked around enough. He wasn't complaining, after all, he had had a tremendous stroke of luck with his business. But he'd seen enough hard times to want to just settle in and live. Just he, his daughter, his business and his memories. He didn't want any more complications, any more involvements. "No, I'd better be going."

Chicken. She turned to face him, her back against the door. "I had a very good time, Shea."

The evening breeze shifted, bringing her perfume to him. Stirring him. "Glad you enjoyed it."

"And I appreciate you telling me what you did." She tilted her head up, her eyes on his. "I know it wasn't easy for you."

"Someday," Shea said, drawing her into his arms because he couldn't seem to help himself. "Someone is going to punch you in that lovely upturned nose of yours for sticking it in the wrong place."

She liked the feeling of his arms around her. She could get used to this. "Then I'll call you to come to my rescue."

He shook his head. "No, I don't think so. I just might applaud."

"No, you wouldn't." Dottie raised up on her toes. "You're definitely the knight-in-shining-armor type."

"Ha." Her mouth was too close, he thought. His resistance was dissolving.

"Never say 'ha' to a psychologist." Her eyes danced. "It undermines their self-confidence."

"Nothing could undermine your confidence."

"Don't be so sure." She placed her hands on his arms. They felt strong, protective. A woman could feel safe here. "You haven't kissed me good-night, yet."

No, he hadn't. And he wanted to. There was no getting away from that. "Easily remedied." He bent his head and kissed her.

He should have known that he couldn't just kiss her and leave. There was no such thing as just a kiss. Not with her. It was a sensual experience that drugged his senses and totally blocked out all shreds of common sense. He wanted to hold her forever, kiss her forever. Make love with her until it totally blotted out all traces of the guilt that ate away at his soul like water wearing away a rock over the course of time.

Dottie allowed herself to fall into the kiss without thought of resistance or what the consequences might be. She simply felt and enjoyed as her knees weakened from the impact. Instinctively, she knew that there was never going to be anyone else for her again.

His lips left hers all too soon. She held on for a moment longer, slightly dazed. "That certainly restores my confidence."

"And wreaks total havoc on mine." He smiled as he left her on the doorstep. He wasn't walking all too surefootedly himself.

By the end of the second week, Shea saw a definite change taking place in his daughter. A certain poise was beginning to seep in, a confidence without the tomboyishness that had always been attached to it before. Each evening at dinner, Al recited what she and Dottie had done that day. It was no longer "what Dottie taught me" but what she and Dottie had experienced together. Dottie was going about the matter of transforming his boisterous little girl into a young lady subtly, even though the girl had asked for this. He had to admire Dottie's methods.

He had to admire a lot about Dottie McClellan, he thought as he let himself into the house that Friday evening. Not the least of which seemed to be her spirit.

"So. I'll be seeing you on Monday, Al," Dottie picked up her purse and prepared to leave. "Unless..." Dottie stopped and turned as Shea walked into the living room.

"Unless what?" Shea asked as he placed his briefcase on the coffee table. He knew he had walked into a setup the moment he looked into Dottie's eyes. Knew it and somehow didn't seem to mind.

"Unless you'd like to come for Sunday dinner at Mama Marino's," Dottie concluded.

Her family. He didn't think he was ready for something like that. Not if they were all like Dottie, and he had a sneaking suspicion that they were. "I'm afraid I don't think we can—" He caught the hopeful expression on Al's face and stopped.

"Please, Dad?" Al put her hands on his arm and tugged, as if that would get him to change his mind. "Dottie's been telling me about Frankie."

"Frankie?" Shea looked at Dottie. "And just who is Frankie?"

"My nephew. You know, J.T.'s son."

Shea crossed his arms before his chest as he eyed her. "Planning to marry her off as well as teach her about classical music?"

Dottie let Al field that one. She had told the girl enough about Frankie for her to manage on her own. "He plays baseball really well, Dad."

"Still interested in baseball?" Shea tugged on a lock of curly hair. He didn't know why, but the fact that she still liked baseball was comforting for some reason. He realized that he wasn't quite as prepared for his daughter's transition as he thought he was.

"Oh, Dad." Al gave her father an impatient frown. "Dottie says there's no harm in a lady participating in sports."

"Oh, she does, does she?" He looked at Dottie over his shoulder. Smart lady, Dottie. Silently, he blessed her. Louisa, he knew, would have made Al feel like a mutant for wanting to play baseball. "Well, she's right."

"Then can we go?" Al asked eagerly.

Dottie, he thought, was oddly quiet during this exchange. "How did we get from A to B?"

"Dazzling footwork," Dottie put in with a grin.

Shea draped an arm around Al's shoulders. "Teach her that, too?"

"I didn't have to," Dottie informed him. She winked at Al. "It's inherent in the species."

"Thanks for the warning."

His survivor's instinct, which had seen him through so much before, warned him that this was not a good move. Going to Mama Marino's for a family dinner would only get him further entrenched, deeper into the trap he wanted to avoid at all costs.

But the imploring look on Al's face negated his common sense. He told himself he was saying yes for Al's sake. Shea ran his hand over the back of his neck. "I guess there's no harm in going, if your mother doesn't mind two extra mouths to feed."

"Mind?" Dottie laughed at the idea. "The woman lives to feed. Don't eat any breakfast," she warned, patting Shea's stomach. "I'll be here at eleven. Wear something to play ball in," she told Al. The girl beamed with relief at the mandate.

Dottie walked into her apartment in time to hear the telephone ringing above the chorus of greetings she received at her front door.

"Yes, I'm glad to see you, too." The dogs surrounded her on all three sides. "Now clear a path so I can get to the phone."

She hurried to the telephone and grabbed it on the fourth ring. "Hello?" Dottie sank down on the sofa and kicked off her shoes, getting comfortable.

"Dottie, it's J.T."

"Ah, my elusive accountant sister-in-law. Where've you been for the last week? I've been trying to get a hold of you."

"I'm sorry. It's just that—"

Dottie cut through her apology. "It's okay." She rubbed one foot against the arch of the other. Waldo scurried back and forth, chasing her toes. "I have some of the answers I needed."

"Dottie."

J.T.'s tone of voice brought Dottie's chatter to a halt. "What's up, J.T.? You sound awful." She wasn't prepared for what J.T. blurted out next.

"Dottie, I'm pregnant."

The words had come out in a wail, but Dottie hardly heard. She sat up, her tired feet forgotten. "Wow, that's wonderful."

J.T. didn't sound as if that was the word she had in mind. "Dottie, I'm too old to start all over again."

Dottie laughed. J.T. was only thirty-four. "Obviously not."

"Frankie's fourteen."

"So, you've got a built-in baby-sitter."

J.T. sighed loudly. "Can't get any sympathy from you, can I?"

"Not a whit." A baby. Dottie could hardly wait. "I think it's fantastic. How far along are you?"

"Three months. I guess it's fantastic, too. It's just that I suppose I'm nervous." She paused. "Will you hold my hand if I get cranky?"

"Try and stop me." Howard poked his snout at her arm. Dottie began scratching him behind the ear absently. "How's Shad taking it?"

"Like he's the first one who's ever done it."

She could hear the grin in J.T.'s voice. Dottie laughed. "Yes, that's Shad, all right. Have you told Mama yet?"

"No. You're the first one outside of Shad and Frankie. Think she'll be excited?"

"Excited? Is the Pope Catholic? I know, make the announcement tomorrow at dinner. She'll be thrilled to death." Maybe on two counts, Dottie thought. "Oh, by the way." She tried to sound nonchalant, but she knew she wasn't succeeding very well. "I'm bringing Shea and his daughter tomorrow."

"Oh."

Dottie knew smug when she heard it. "Now *that's* a pregnant 'oh.'"

"It's just that you hardly ever bring anyone to dinner."

J.T. sounded unusually pleased with the turn of events. "I thought that getting together at Mama's would be good for them. Shea needs to be brought out a little."

"I thought you were working with Al."

There was something too innocent about the remark. Dottie was beginning to smell a rat. "Al's coming along beautifully."

"And Shea?"

She thought of his reluctance to come in for a drink after dinner last Sunday. "Needs coaxing."

"Then it's serious."

There was no point in trying to be evasive. J.T. was family and Dottie was always open about her feelings. "It could be, given the right circumstances."

"Which are?"

"Well, he needs to get over whatever it is that's bothering him." Dottie tried to keep the frustration she felt out of her voice. "I can't get Shea to talk to me about it."

J.T. laughed softly. "You? You could get a clam to talk, Dottie."

She thought of the dinner they had shared. "Well, he's told me about how he got started in the antique business."

"You know more than I do. And I've known him for five years."

"But I can't get him to tell me anything about his wife." And that, she felt, was where all their problems were.

"It's a very sore point. She died before I became his accountant. I did hear that it was some sort of a car accident that Shea blamed himself for."

Dottie dragged her hand through her hair. "That might explain his resistance to getting involved with anyone." But why did he blame himself? Had he been the one driving when she died?

"I'd like to see him get involved with you. Everyone needs a whirlwind in their lives at least once. I think you'd be good for him."

Dottie laughed and shook her head. "Now you're beginning to talk like Mama."

"Really?" J.T. asked innocently. "I haven't mentioned making alterations on your wedding gown."

"Not mine," Dottie corrected. "*Her* wedding gown, J.T. *Her* wedding gown." She leaned her back against the side of the sofa and hung her hand over the side. She felt something wet and looked to see which of the dogs was licking her fingers.

"She wants to see you wear it."

Dottie pulled her hand back. "I can model it for her any Sunday."

"At St. Joseph's."

"Sure," Dottie laughed, "why not?"

"With a priest in attendance," J.T. added pointedly.

"Now it's getting complicated."

"Maybe not. I happen to think that Shea Delany would make an excellent husband. He's got a lot to offer a woman."

They were in agreement on that point. "Too bad he doesn't think so."

"Have you kissed him?"

She had always wanted a big sister to talk about things like this. It felt a little odd, though, starting at twenty-seven. "Yes, I've kissed him."

"And?"

Dottie heard the eagerness in J.T.'s voice. "There is no 'and', J.T." Dottie sighed. "I've only kissed the man."

That wasn't fair. There was no "only" in front of that statement. She'd kissed him and seen stars and rainbows and all the stereotypical things she didn't think really happened to people. Until they had happened to her.

"I know you, Dottie. You wouldn't be bringing him to dinner tomorrow to endure Mama's scrutiny if you had 'only' kissed him. C'mon, where did it register on the Richter scale?"

Dottie leaned back even farther and closed her eyes, remembering. She curled her toes. "Twelve."

"Ah-ha."

Dottie scrambled back up into a sitting position. She still had things to do. Enough flights of fantasy for one evening. "Save your 'ah-ha' for a while."

"I'm willing to bet not too long a while. I've never known you to let grass grow under your feet, Dottie. Or have dust accumulate, except maybe behind you as you go charging off."

Dottie laughed at the imagery as she looked around for her shoes. "That sounds like a stunning character reference."

"I wouldn't have sent him to you if I didn't believe that maybe—"

Dottie stopped, holding her other shoe in her hand. "Were you playing matchmaker?"

She would have never believed it of her sister-in-law. Maybe it came from associating with Mama over these last two years. Mama wanted nothing more than to have all her children married with children of their own. And all eating dinner at her table on Sunday.

"Maybe just a little," J.T. conceded, obviously recognizing the error of letting the cat out of the bag. "I knew you could help him with what he had in mind for Al." J.T.'s voice picked up speed. "And the fact that you're both unattached and charming didn't exactly dissuade me from the decision either."

"You know, I was wrong," Dottie said slowly.

"About what?"

"You." She tried to sound serious, but she was too pleased to carry it off very well. She was glad J.T. had done what she had. It had brought a fascinating man into her life. "I didn't think you were devious, J.T."

"I'm not. I'm just concerned."

"A likely story. Go eat some pickles and ice cream."

"Please, don't mention food."

She could almost hear J.T. turning green over the phone. "How are you going to survive tomorrow?"

"Maybe if I tell Mama as soon as I get there," J.T. said hopefully, "she'll excuse me."

"Excuse you? Are we talking about the same woman? You tell her you're pregnant and she'll be loading your plate up for two."

J.T. groaned.

Chapter Nine

"So." Bridgette Marino clasped her hands together as she slowly and deliberately looked Shea up and down, regarding him in the same manner a careful shopper peruses a contemplated acquisition. "This is the man who likes action."

Shea stood on Bridgette Marino's doorstep, one hand placed lightly on his daughter's shoulder. He felt very much like a fish out of water as he gave Dottie a quizzical look. Just *what* had she said to this woman?

"Auctions, Mama," Dottie corrected patiently, though she knew it probably made no lasting impression. Mama spoke her own brand of English and got by very nicely, thank you very much, she had said to Dottie more than once. "Shea likes auctions, not action."

Off the hook, Shea grinned engagingly. "That's not entirely true," he murmured under his breath to Dottie.

The comment surprised them both. It was more in keeping with something he would have said years ago. When he

had felt freer, more reckless. Before there had been respon-
sibilities to shoulder. She seemed to have a way of bringing
those feelings out of him again, even though he thought they
were long buried.

"Mrs. Marino." With a flourish, Shea took the older
woman's hand and kissed it. "It's a pleasure to finally meet
you. Dottie has told me a great deal about you."

Dottie wouldn't have thought it was possible, but she saw
Bridgette Marino blush to the roots of her salt-and-pepper
hair, even though the woman looked at Shea knowingly.
"He flirts well, this one," Bridgette commented to Dottie.

Dottie laughed, pleased. She looked at Shea. "I think she
likes you."

Mama spread her hands wide. "He is young, he is handsome and he is here. What is not to like?"

Not a darn thing, Dottie thought with a grin.

"I'm beginning to understand where you get your out-
spokenness from," Shea confided.

Mama turned her attention to Al, who was shifting a little uncomfortably at Shea's side. She seemed uncertain
whether to act the perfect young lady or to give in to the
feeling generated by her casual clothes and revert, for the
space of the day, back to the tomboy she still enjoyed being.

Mama read the dilemma in Al's eyes and smiled. "You
will be yourself here," she instructed benevolently, patting
the girl's hand.

Shea noticed the pleased expression on his daughter's
face. "Mrs. Marino, may I present my daughter, Alessandra."

Al wrinkled her nose mechanically at the sound of her full
name.

"Alessandra." On Mama's tongue, it sounded like a
melody. "What a beautiful name. Come." Mama slipped

her soft hand into the young girl's. "I have something for you."

Dottie leaned her head toward Shea. "Food," she whispered knowingly. She threaded her arm through his, leading him into the house. Once, it had been constructed in railroad fashion, one room lined up behind the other. But Papa had fixed that, adding on slowly, making it spread out like an aging, contented patriarch. Now the house had an open, cheery appearance.

"You were very charming." Dottie patted his arm. "She ate it up."

He looked at her skeptically. "She wasn't fooled for a moment."

Dottie laughed in agreement. "No, she wasn't. Mama always has a way of seeing through deception. But she was still charmed. Maybe what she saw was real," Dottie suggested.

Shea looked around the room as they entered. It was exactly what he had expected, what he would have loved to have claimed as his own home when he was growing up. The furniture was old but sturdy. The room crowded with memories and love. And one wall, next to the fireplace, was devoted to framed photographs of the family. Without thinking, he wandered over to it.

"Meaning?" he picked out one photograph of a pigtailed young girl buffered on either side by rough-and-tumble-looking little boys. Even then, there was mischief in her eyes.

"That the true Shea Delany is somewhere between the streetwise boy unjustly convicted and the subdued man of good taste who owns a chain of antique stores and attends 'actions.'" He turned to look at her. "A hybrid. The best of both."

His expression grew grim. "There was no best in the streetwise kid." Everyone had always said that. He was looked down upon then, called names he wouldn't repeat. By the time he was twelve, he had long since lost count of the fights he had been in, defending his mother's name against what he prayed were vicious lies.

Dottie wasn't about to let Shea belittle his worth. "He pulled himself out of his environment, didn't he?"

Shea shoved his hands into his pockets. "Yes, but—"

She ran right over his protest. "That took guts and cunning."

He laughed. "Maybe I should hire you as my public relations agent." He noticed another photograph, a professional one taken in a studio. J.T.'s wedding. Dottie was her maid of honor, dressed in a soft pink gown with flowers in her hair. He wished he could have been there to pick them out, one by one.

"I only speak the truth, remember?" She looked over his shoulder to see what had caught his attention. It made her smile. "I don't beat around the bush."

Shea moved away from the wall of photographs, from the memories that weren't his to share. "You're supposed to work on my daughter, not me."

"I can't help myself. It's like eating one potato chip." She shrugged. "I see something that needs doing and I have to do it."

"I don't need 'doing' and I never thought of myself as a potato chip." He looked at her, trying to maintain a stern expression. "Some people would call that meddling."

Dottie merely grinned. It obviously didn't bother her what people called it. "Maybe."

"Shea, you came."

Shea turned around as J.T. entered the room. She looked both pleased and surprised to see him there. "Dottie said she had invited you. I had to see it for myself to believe it."

Shea took both her hands in his, bonding momentarily with a friend against something he didn't yet understand and perhaps feared. He wasn't ready to have his barriers broken down by these people, even though Dottie and Mrs. Marino had other thoughts on the matter. They represented everything he would have wanted as a child. But seeing all this now brought back painful memories, making him feel both angry and sad at the same time. He didn't want to consciously face his reactions. "You look radiant."

J.T. grinned. "There's a reason for that."

"Have you told her?" Dottie pressed.

J.T. nodded. "Didn't you hear the 'Ah, my prayers have been answered!' exclamation? I thought for sure everyone heard it for three city blocks. Angelo's making plans to buy a video camera. We'll probably have to post a guard to keep him out of the delivery room."

"Delivery room," Shea echoed. "Then you're—"

"The medical term is pregnant," J.T. said. "The layman's term is nauseous." She turned as she sensed Shad's presence behind her. "Shea, you know my husband."

The two men regarded each other in silence for a moment, as if sizing one another up for the first time. Then Shad offered his hand to Shea, adding, "I'm Dottie's brother."

"He already knows that, Shad." Dottie patted her brother's cheek. "C'mon, Mama won't forgive me if I don't get you some wine."

She took Shea's hand and led him into the kitchen. Bridgette was holding court there, all by herself. A chorus of pots simmered on the stove in attendance as Bridgette sampled, frowned and added last-minute ingredients.

"Is it my imagination," Shea asked, "or was I just issued a warning?"

Dottie took a tall, unlabeled bottle from the refrigerator and poured Shea a glass of red wine. She handed it to him. "Shad doesn't get much of a chance to act the big brother role. Just humor him. Ask him about my dowry."

Shea almost choked as the wine, smooth and tangy, threatened to come back up. "What?"

She slapped him on the back twice. "Just kidding."

Or half kidding, she added silently. "That's Mama's own recipe. Like it?"

"Yes." That would explain the flavor he couldn't place.

She heard the back door open and close again and turned just as Angelo entered the kitchen. He stole a freshly peeled apple slice from the counter and received a slap on his hand from Bridgette. His grin was amiable and guileless as he popped the slice into his mouth.

"This," Dottie gestured toward the apple thief, "is my other brother, the cuddly teddy bear." She hooked her arms through Angelo's and grinned affectionately.

"Angelo to everyone else." Angelo flashed a quick grin as he took Shea's hand and shook it. "How did she rope you into this?"

"Through fancy footwork and cunning," Shea answered wryly.

Angelo seemed to understand exactly what Shea meant. He'd been there a time or two himself with Dottie. "She does talk fast, doesn't she?" Dottie shot him an indignant look which he appeared to totally ignore. "Doesn't leave much space for a man to sort things out."

"He's doing just fine, thank you very much," Dottie sniffed. "Why don't you make yourself useful and pitch a few balls to Frank?"

"Can't." Angelo jerked a thumb toward the far end of the yard. "It looks as if I've been replaced."

Dottie looked out the back window and grinned. So that was what Mama had meant when she had said she had "something" for Al. She'd meant a kindred spirit. Frankie and Al were in the backyard, totally engrossed in a game of catch and in fashioning a new friendship.

Shea placed a hand on her shoulder as he looked out as well. "See?" Dottie turned around to look at him. "She isn't growing up nearly as fast as you were afraid she was."

Shea stared at Dottie. "How did you know?" How had she known what was going through his mind? How had she sensed that bittersweet pang he felt over the thought of eventually losing Al?

"I'm supposed to know." Her tone was matter-of-fact. "I'm a psychologist." She saw Angelo retreating into the other room. Probably to grill J.T. with some more questions about the baby-to-be. Angelo loved being an uncle. Poor J.T. "And a woman."

Shea looked at the way her hair framed her face like a wayward blond cloud. No matter where he stood in the room, her scent followed him, reminding him that he wanted her, even here in her mother's kitchen. "Yes, I noticed."

Dottie swallowed. The look in his eyes made her mouth go dry. "I know it's hard to let go of something. Of someone."

A lid clattered against a pot and they both jumped. "Hey, you two," Mama pointed to the door with her paring knife, "get some air. You are getting under my feet."

Dottie tugged on his arm. "I think she's trying to tell us we're underfoot. You've saved me, you know," she confided, lowering her voice.

Shea raised an eyebrow. "How so?"

God, he was sexy, she thought as her body tingled in response to his expression. She had to stop to collect her train of thought. "Usually, Mama recruits me to peel potatoes or shell peas or something equally as tedious. She's never shooed me out of the kitchen before." She took a deep breath as she opened the door. "Ah, freedom. It feels wonderful."

She made him laugh again. She was filling his world with laughter. "Glad to be of service." He held the door open for her as she stepped outside into the yard.

A large, yellow awning kept the sun at bay, away from the back of the house. She sat down on the swing seat at the edge of the patio, waiting for him to join her.

When he did, she gestured toward Frankie and Al at the far end of the yard. They were laughing as they pitched the softball back and forth. "They seem to be enjoying themselves," Shea observed.

She could hear the slight edge in his voice. He wasn't sure if he approved, she thought. "They both share a passion for baseball."

"Funny word to use in reference to a teenager." He leaned forward. Dottie stopped swinging. "Or maybe not so funny." A serious look came over his face as he remembered himself at around that age. "How old is your nephew?"

She knew exactly what was on his mind. She was willing to bet that mothers had hid their daughters whenever he came around. Or, at least tried to. "Almost fifteen."

Almost fifteen. More than old enough. "Do you think they'll be all right?"

Dottie placed her hand on his arm. She realized that he didn't notice at first. "As long as that ball keeps sailing back and forth, I'd say that you have nothing to worry about."

"Yeah." Not totally convinced, he still kept an eye in his daughter's direction.

He was going to have to work at letting go. "What were you like at that age?"

"Wild. Undisciplined," he answered mechanically. "Going nowhere fast."

Dottie started the swing in motion again. "You certainly got somewhere in a hurry."

He shrugged carelessly. Perhaps too carelessly, Dottie thought. "Just luck. I hated being poor."

But it wasn't just luck. He had done something with the opportunity that had unexpectedly come his way. "Yes, but not everybody does something constructive about it."

Satisfied that his daughter was enjoying herself harmlessly, he looked back at Dottie. "Not everybody hated it as much as I did. Or had a taste of jail."

"Reform school," she corrected automatically, responding to the trace of bitterness in his voice.

Shea forced himself to relax. It was all in the past. "It felt like jail to me. I hate confinement."

She watched as the ball sailed easily from Frankie's hand to Al's. Frankie was purposely holding back. Amazing what a pretty girl could inspire a boy to do. "Is that why you back away from relationships?"

Shea's eyes narrowed. "Boy, you just jump right in there, don't you?"

She fixed him with an innocent smile that no longer fooled him as it once did. "Simpler."

"Blunter."

"That, too."

She was waiting for an answer. "No, jail, or reform school," he amended as she opened her mouth, "has nothing to do with the way I feel about relationships."

She'd come this far, she might as well go all the way. "What does?"

He wanted to tell her, to tell her about Sandra, about the accident. About what had frozen his heart. But he had kept it all in for so long, the words refused to form. "I thought this was supposed to be a pleasant afternoon."

"Sorry." But she wasn't. She was only sorry he wouldn't tell her. "I tend to tread where angels fear to go, as the old song lyric runs."

"Why?" It was his turn to want to know.

"The song lyric runs that way because the composer needed a rhyme." She leaned closer, sincerity in every word she uttered. "I'm that way because I care."

"Care about what?" Maybe if he attacked, she'd retreat. But he had a feeling she wouldn't. The woman refused to act to form.

"People. Al. You."

"Don't." It was only a single word, but it was a warning.

There was a recklessness about her, Shea thought, because she refused to back off. Something else they had in common.

"Why?" Dottie pressed.

"Because it makes it too difficult." Why couldn't she just leave it at that? Why did she have to push—and make him feel that somehow, it might be possible when he knew in his heart that it couldn't be. He couldn't let it.

"Life wasn't meant to be easy." The summer breeze, hot and sultry, picked up and played roughly with the fallen leaves on the patio near her feet. "Easy things are taken for granted. It's the hard-won things that are treasured." She pushed her hair from her face.

A smile curved his mouth as he thought of the way he had felt, opening the doors to his store for the first time. "Yes."

Dottie looked at him. "Like Sandra?"

He was surprised that she knew his wife's name. She could see it in his face.

"J.T. told me your wife's name. I asked."

A flat, distant look entered his eyes that she couldn't read. "Sandra was not that hard to win. She was mine the minute our eyes met on the school campus." An ironic, mirthless smile twisted his lips. "It was getting her away from her mother that was hard."

"Louisa." The woman who had inadvertently brought them together. Al had filled her in on a lot of details over the last two weeks. Dottie didn't care for the woman, or at least she didn't care for the way Louisa had conducted her letter-writing campaign. Al had shown her the letters she had saved. There were subtle attempts to transform Al into the image of her mother through comparisons and hints that Al would be less of a person if she didn't strive to be just like her mother.

Shea nodded. "Louisa."

She could hear anger and loathing in the way he said the woman's name. How much bad blood was there between these two?

Dottie summoned all the gentle, persuasive powers she had as she looked into his eyes. "How did your wife die, Shea?"

"In a car accident." Even the monotone voice did not hide the raw pain that existed beneath.

Mama stuck her head out into the yard. "Dinner, everyone." She clapped her hands, looking at Frankie and Al. "Come now or you will be sorry."

Dottie closed her eyes, frustrated. Shea had already risen to his feet. The moment was gone.

Oh, Mama, your timing couldn't have been worse, Dottie thought.

She rose from the seat. It squeaked as it continued gently swaying. "We'd better go in. She means what she says about the sorry part." With that, Dottie hooked her arm through his and led him inside.

It wasn't until several hours later, after dinner was just a pleasant, satiating memory and Shad and Angelo had gone off to teach Frankie and Al the finer points of billiards in the games room, that Dottie had another opportunity to pick up the threads of their aborted conversation.

She coaxed Shea outside, leaving J.T. at the mercy of Mama's memories and photo albums. Mama was reliving a time when they all had been young. The promise of a baby had sent her back through time for the evening.

Dusk was slowly sneaking in. Shea had no idea how so much time had managed to pass. He had only meant to stay an hour or two. But that had stretched into an entire afternoon and filtered into evening. Al, he knew, was enjoying herself immensely. Growing up without a single aunt or uncle, the idea of sharing a day with a boisterous family that shouted and loved was something the girl absorbed with great alacrity.

If he let himself drift along as well, he could be forgiven just this once. The company, even with Shad's initial hooded, probing looks and guarded conversation, had been pleasant. Shea had eventually found a lot to talk about with Shad and Angelo, a lot in common with men who believed in making their own opportunities, just as he did.

And there was Dottie. He had to admit that he enjoyed being with her, just watching her talk, laugh. Breathe. It was safe here, safe to want her, safe to yearn. He couldn't do anything about it in these circumstances. And it couldn't do anything to him. Couldn't undo him.

Dottie wound her fingers around his hand as they walked about the yard. The cooling evening breeze flitted around flirtatiously. It heightened her mood. "There used to be a badminton court strung up here." She pointed out two rusted poles. "Papa put it up for us one summer. I think we played every night for three months straight."

He envied her. "You were happy here."

"Very." She looked at him. "Were you ever happy?" He looked so sad now. Had everything in his childhood been that way?

"Al makes me happy." Dottie didn't say anything and he knew what she was waiting for. "Her mother made me happy." His voice softened as he remembered. "She was a very special lady."

Dottie's heart ached for him. "You've been in mourning a long time."

"Mourning?" He looked at her as he rolled the word, the thought, over in his mind. "I suppose, in a way, I have."

It seemed almost out of character. "I would have thought you'd be the type who'd get on with his life."

"I did," he said simply. "I built up the business, opened new stores. There was only one store until Sandra died. Louisa was certain I'd married Sandra for her money. She was surprised I didn't build up right after we were married."

"She disapproved of you." It wasn't really a question.

He laughed shortly. "From the very first. She still does."

But he had done so much, tried so hard. "Why?"

"Isn't it obvious?" Shea shoved his hands into his pockets as he moved about the yard restlessly. "I was born on the wrong side. Sandra had ancestors going back to the Founding Fathers. Louisa thought I was after that, after that kind of respectability. And don't forget the money." He shook his head. How could something so sweet have been born to a woman so bitter? "She was sure that no one could love Sandra just for her own sake."

"But you did." And she suddenly realized that she loved him for that. Loved him for his heart that no one had ever understood, for his bravery against all odds. Loved him for the man he had been as well as the one he had fought to become.

"Yes, I did. I didn't want the money. Just her. She made it all worthwhile somehow. If only—" His voice trailed off as he listened to the call of a night bird. He turned back when he felt her hand on his arm.

"If only?" Dottie encouraged.

If only she had been more like you. "If only she hadn't been so afraid of her mother, of what Louisa'd think, or say." He was tempted to say something further, to voice his anger, but he bit back the words. It would serve no purpose. Sandra was gone. Dottie took his hand in hers.

It seemed to bring him back. "You're easy to talk to." He ran his hand through her hair. So silky, so delicate. Like her mouth.

"I'm glad."

He threaded both hands through her hair, cupping the back of her head. "Why are you messing around with my mind, Dottie?"

She tilted her head, relishing the feel of his stronger fingers on her neck, anticipating his mouth. "I'm just trying to get some answers, Shea."

He shook his head. He had already told her too much. "They're not your questions to ask."

She smiled. "There we seem to have a difference of opinion."

"What makes your opinion right?" he challenged. "And what," he breathed, moving his hand so that he could run his thumb along her lower lip, "makes you so damn attractive to me?"

"The right toothpaste?"

When things were light, she would say something serious. And when they were serious, like now, she'd find a quip to put things into perspective. "You make me laugh, Dottie."

"Always a good thing." Her eyes held his, afraid to move.

He drew her closer to his face. "And you make me want."

"Not a bad trait, either," she whispered, waiting.

"No, bad. Very bad."

"Why?"

"Because."

He had no more words than that, no more power left to him than to utter it. All his concentration had left him. The only driving force in his life at this very moment was to kiss her, to press her against his wanting body and savor the heat of hers throughout his system.

His lips trailed along her face, branding her, changing the course of her life forever and making her his whether or not he wanted her. She knew that she would always belong to him.

Dottie's hands tightened on his arms as the passion she felt rekindled, flaming high and igniting him, making him weak, taking him prisoner. He couldn't call any of the shots. Again. Control was no longer his. And it worried him.

"That's a hell of an argument against you," she breathed. She leaned her cheek against his chest, trying to compose herself. She felt his ragged breathing and smiled to herself.

He was shaken. She kept doing that to him, kept playing with his emotions and feelings and making him veer from the path he knew he should stick to. The only path that was safe.

Abruptly, he took her hand. "C'mon, your mother's going to be insulted if we stay out here too long." He turned for the house.

Dottie followed. His words didn't fool her. It wasn't her mother he was worried about. It was himself. "On the contrary, she's probably planning on making alterations right now."

"Alterations?" Shea looked at her over his shoulder, confused.

"Private joke," she murmured as she walked into the kitchen. "I'll explain it to you someday." *Maybe someday very soon.*

Chapter Ten

Though he had thrown himself into his business after Sandra had died, Shea had always made it a point not to stay late at work unless it was an emergency. To do so, to allow work to take over his life that way, would have cut into his time with Al. More than anything else, he didn't want to shortchange his daughter.

But now he had another reason to look forward to coming home. He knew that Dottie would be there.

And since he knew that the situation was only temporary, he felt more able to enjoy it without the fear of consequences hanging over his head. With Al and Athena there, they kept him from acting on his feelings. In a way, he was tightrope walking *with* a net. Once Louisa came and hopefully went, Al wouldn't feel the need to continue this *blitzkrieg* approach to absorbing culture. She'd be satisfied to learn more slowly.

Besides, school wasn't that far off. Her studies would take priority. And Dottie would go back to her own life, to es-

tablishing her career. They would go their separate ways all
too soon.

It made what he felt was happening between them now
easier to excuse, he thought. He was a normal, healthy male
and he was reacting to her. It was a passing reaction, just
one of those things. Perhaps it even fell into the realm of
infatuation. But nothing more. He would enjoy what was
happening, knowing that nothing permanent would evolve.
He wouldn't let it. He couldn't risk making another mistake that could wind up destroying someone's life.

You didn't play with fire unless you wanted to get burned.

He wasn't playing. He had only flicked the lighter on. He
knew how to control it, how to shut it off. Under no circumstances would he let it catch hold of anything, least of
all him.

With all that carefully arranged in his mind, Shea unlocked the front door and walked in.

"They are in the living room," Athena announced when
he had taken no more than two steps into the house. "See
what you can do about getting her to abandon that pig of
hers for an evening and eat here. Dinner is in five minutes,
so be quick about it, Mr. Shea."

He wondered at times who paid whose salary. But he
knew this wasn't about who was in whose employ. This was
about caring.

Shea went into the living room and found both Dottie and
Al sitting on the floor by the coffee table. "So," he looked
at the scene, so natural that it stirred a longing within him,
"what's on the agenda for tomorrow?"

Al scrambled up from the floor when she saw him. Her
hand hit the videos stacked on the coffee table. Like the
Tower of Babel, they fell and haphazardly went sliding
along the highly polished surface.

Shea stooped to pick up the video that had landed at his feet. He glanced at the title on the case. It was about the life of Émile Zola. He looked quizzically at Dottie. "What's this?"

"Biographies," Al announced as she took it from him and placed it back on the table.

"It's faster than reading," Dottie added. She took the hand he offered and rose to her feet.

"And not nearly as accurate," Shea pointed out. "These things take a lot of liberties with the truth."

"So do books at times," Dottie countered, unfazed. "Besides, this'll be fun."

Everything seemed to be fun with her around, he thought, though he kept it to himself. No use in letting the woman feel totally confident.

He picked up another video and read the title aloud. *"Lust for Life?"*

She could see by his expression that he wasn't too thrilled about the title, at least not as far as his daughter was concerned. "The life of Vincent van Gogh. Kirk Douglas." Dottie took the video tape from him and placed it on top of the pile. "Tame stuff."

Al tossed her head, her hands on her hips and struck the eternal stance of defiance against parental censorship. "Dad, I'm old enough to see things."

He laughed, breaking the mood, as he ruffled her hair. Al attempted to look annoyed, but failed miserably. Clearly, part of her still liked being Daddy's little girl. Part of her always would.

"Yes, but I'm not old enough to watch you seeing them." Shea turned to Dottie. "Why don't we get started after dinner?"

He wasn't about to get an argument from her on that. "Is that an invitation?"

"Absolutely." He nodded toward the dining room. "I'm tired of listening to Athena grumble because you have to go home to a pig."

Dottie laughed in response. "Well, then she won't have anything to grumble about tonight."

"She'll find something," Shea promised Dottie as they walked out. "She always does."

"Um, Dottie?" Al began hesitantly.

"Yes?" As Dottie looked at the girl, she felt a pang. She was going to miss being with her every day when this was all over. Al was sweet and dear and on her way to becoming a stunning young woman.

"Could I come over your house tomorrow and see Howard again?" Al cast one eye in Shea's direction to see if that met with his approval.

"I can't think of anything I'd like better." Dottie placed an arm around the girl's shoulders and gave her a quick hug. "And Howard loves the attention."

"So." Athena stood in the doorway of the kitchen, her thin face drawn into a scowl. "This one, she is finally staying?"

Shea held out a chair for Dottie. "Your sweet disposition convinced her."

"I do not know why I stay here and take this abuse,". Athena muttered audibly as she went to get another place setting.

Al grinned broadly. "Because you love us," she called after Athena.

"Don't be so sure of yourself, young one," Athena warned as the swinging door closed behind her.

"She reminds me a lot of Mama Marino," Dottie told Shea. "Maybe the need to boss people around has something to do with being petite. Like Napoleon."

Shea smiled and nodded his thanks as Athena brought out another plate and silverware. "How tall did you say you were?" he asked Dottie.

She lifted her chin proudly. "I'm not petite. I'm just under-tall. Thank you, Athena."

"Humph. 'Bout time you sat down and had a decent meal here," Athena grunted, but her eyes smiled at Dottie as she went back to the kitchen.

"With an answer for everything," Shea commented on Dottie's assessment of her height.

"Can I help, Athena?" Dottie called after the woman, half-rising from her chair.

"You sit right there," Athena ordered, returning with a large serving bowl, "and don't you be getting in my way. That'll be help enough."

"That puts me in my place," Dottie murmured, sitting down again.

"I doubt it," Shea replied.

"If you're referring to my energetic manner, growing up with two brothers did that to me." She accepted the bowl of mashed potatoes that Shea passed to her. "The runt of the litter never survives without some sort of an edge."

He couldn't picture her being the runt of any litter. "You talk as if you came from my kind of neighborhood."

"Being an orphan means coming from the poorest, roughest neighborhood there is," she told him matter-of-factly. She saw that Al had stopped eating and was listening in rapt attention. "You've got a lot going against you as an orphan, not the least of which is a stigma." She glanced at Al. "You can let that get to you, or you can overcome it."

"And you overcame it." There was more than a trace of adulation in Al's voice.

She wasn't about to take more than her share of credit. "I had the greatest foster parents ever created on the face of

this earth." She grew more serious as she looked at Shea.
"But you never quite forget the hand that fate dealt you."

Shea thought of Sandra, of the short time they had had
together. And of the reason why. "No." His mouth was
grim. "You never do."

What was it he wasn't telling her? Dottie glanced at Al.
He definitely wasn't going to elaborate in front of his
daughter. She felt certain that he wasn't talking about his
roots, but about something else. Something more. It was the
same untouchable subject that was a barrier between them
as surely as if there was a locked, steel door standing there.

"We went to the art museum again today," Dottie said
abruptly, feeling the need to change topics. She saw a
grateful, relieved expression cross Shea's face.

You're off the hook now, but not forever, Dottie thought.

"I've decided I don't like Kandinsky after all," Al told
her father. "I like the collected works of Monet much better. Dottie showed them to me in a book."

Shea tried to hide the smile that came to his lips. He exchanged looks with Dottie. "Whatever happened to 'I think
that picture's pretty'?" At the beginning of the summer Al
would have had to have been dragged to the art museum
kicking and screaming, now she was talking about "collected works."

Al fingered a strand of her hair, tugging on it. "Oh Dad,
that's for children."

This time he let the teasing expression flower across his
face. "You went through puberty in three weeks?"

Al threw her shoulders back, flustered and at a loss for a
response. "Dad-dee."

Dottie came to her rescue and received an almost ador-
ing look from the girl. "A woman is allowed to change her
mind," Dottie interjected. "It's part of our inalienable
rights."

Al frowned, confused. "What does that mean?"

Shea cut Dottie off. Not an easy thing, he surmised. "It means you're allowed to drive men crazy any time you want to."

"It doesn't—does it?" Al looked at Dottie for confirmation.

"Rather loosely put, but yes." Dottie laughed. Did she drive him crazy? She hoped so, just a little. Just in the area that counted. "There is a lot of truth in that explanation."

He liked the way Dottie tilted her head when she laughed. Sandra had always been so timidly serious, so precious in her uncertainty. He had wanted to wrap her up in tissue paper and protect her. Dottie didn't generate feelings like that within him. He didn't want to wrap Dottie up, except perhaps in his arms.

There was no "perhaps" about it. He wanted to hold her, to kiss her, to see her eyes open wide in passion, to feel her skin beneath his fingers, to explore every inch of her body until he knew it better than his own.

"Not eating much tonight I see, Mr. Shea."

Shea stared as he suddenly realized that Athena was standing at his elbow. He had drifted off for a moment.

He raised his hands to allow the woman access to his plate. "No appetite."

Athena cleared away Shea's place setting, her face absolutely straight. "Mmm-hmm."

She was smirking with a straight face. He knew her subtle body language well enough by now. He was even more convinced he was right when he saw the pleased look on Dottie's face. Shea rested his arms on the table, steepling his fingers before him. The best defense in this case was diversion. "Looks like you had a busy day. The art museum this morning and a film festival planned for this evening."

"Al was interested in van Gogh and liked some of the scenes depicted by Gauguin." Dottie smiled and nodded as Athena motioned to her plate. The woman swept it away. "I thought it might be fun for her to see a movie about the men. I used to love to watch biographies as a kid."

He could almost envision it. The pigtailed young girl he had seen in the photographs in Bridgette Marino's living room, lying on her stomach before a huge television with a small screen, her head propped up on her hands, completely captivated by what she saw.

"Well, then we'll have to do this up right." Pushing himself away from the table, Shea rose to his feet and helped Dottie with her chair. "We'll watch in the video room."

She thought she detected a sentimental look on his face. What was he thinking about? "Most people just have a video machine, you have a video room?"

It did seem like a bit much, but he had to admit he enjoyed the trappings that success brought. "The previous owner put it in. A retired film star who liked to spend hours watching himself on the screen, the realtor told me when I bought this house."

"You'll like it," Al promised as she grabbed Dottie's hand and pulled her toward the room. "It's just like going to the movies."

Dottie made a detour to the living room and grabbed the top two videos on the pile. The video room was located upstairs, just beyond Al's bedroom. The drapes were drawn, enveloping the room in darkness. She had to admit that it did remind her a little of a movie theater.

"This is very impressive." Dottie looked around the room as Shea turned on one standing, long-necked lamp. Unlike the other rooms this one didn't have a single antique in it. The furnishings were all modern. The rectangular sofa was of soft, tan Italian leather, perfect for sitting back and viewing movies.

Or for talking away long, lazy Sunday afternoons, she thought, looking at Shea.

When he caught her at it, Dottie raised the video in her hand aloft. "Let the videos begin."

An hour and a half later, an exhausted Al fell asleep watching van Gogh agonize over his wretched life and his lack of success.

Dottie looked at the blond head that rested on her shoulder. "Maybe this wasn't such a good idea," she murmured to Shea.

Shea leaned forward and took in the scene for a moment. It gave him a contented feeling that he couldn't quite put into words. He was afraid that if he did, it would fade away.

He smiled at Dottie and she could feel desire unfurling in her stomach like a mischievous kitten stretching after a long nap.

"Oh, I don't know. She doesn't usually fall asleep this early, but once she does, she sleeps like a rock until morning. One of her best traits when she was a baby. Let me get her to bed." He rose with his daughter in his arms. "Will you stay?"

You'd have to blast me out. "I won't move a muscle."

But she did. As soon as he had left, she found she was too restless to sit and contemplate Kirk Douglas in a rust-colored beard.

"Sorry, Kirk. I have plans for this VCR." She hit the rewind button and the image vanished from the screen, to be replaced by a monotone weatherman predicting another day of glorious sunshine in the Southland. When she heard the click that signaled the tape had been rewound to the beginning, she ejected it and placed another movie video in its stead.

"You moved."

She turned from the VCR to see him standing in the doorway, framed by the light from the hall. He looked more like the man she imagined he had been, trying to turn life to his advantage. Dark, dangerous. Sexy. She felt the pulse in her throat pick up speed. "Only to put on another video."

He sat down on the sofa, his eyes never leaving her. "Whose life are we going to be watching?"

"No one's." Dottie pressed the play button, then closed the video box and replaced it on the coffee table. "I rented *Casablanca*."

"You're an old movie buff, too?"

She returned *Lust for Life* to its case. "Movies are an art form and I love all forms of art. Especially old movies where everyone always dressed well and they fade out to the beach or the sky at crucial moments." Her eyes twinkled as she said it.

She sat down on the sofa next to him, curling her feet under her. She had the knack, he thought, of making herself comfortable almost instantly no matter what the situation. He found himself wishing that he felt half as comfortable as she looked. He had never felt nervous around a woman before. He felt nervous now.

Shea watched the way she toyed with the ends of her hair. Maybe she wasn't quite as calm as she was letting on. It heartened him. "You're an interesting person, Dottie McClellan."

"So are you."

It would be easy, so easy, just to rest her head on his shoulder, to let herself drift. And feel. But there were still things she needed to know, questions that needed answering. In the background, credits were beginning to slowly scroll as the familiar theme song grew louder.

"Shea," she bit her lower lip, "are you worried about your mother-in-law coming to see Al?"

It was the last thing Shea had expected her to ask. "What makes you think so?"

Dottie noticed that he hadn't answered her question. "Little things. The way your jaw tightens every time her name is mentioned."

He didn't want to talk about Louisa, especially not now. "I tell you what, I won't try to sell you on antiques tonight and you don't try to analyze me." He leaned forward and took a handful of popcorn that Athena had insisted on making. "Deal?" He moved the bowl of popcorn toward her.

She took one kernel and rolled it around in her fingertips. "I wasn't trying to analyze you. I was trying to get to understand you better."

Shea took the kernel from her fingers and placed it in her mouth. The imprint of her lips stayed on his fingers and lingered on his mind. "Isn't that the same thing?"

She felt warm as she watched his eyes. "No. One's professional, the other's personal."

Shea moved the back of his hand along her cheek. The slope was so inviting he felt he had no choice. But his words didn't match his actions. "Don't get too close, Dottie."

This when she was all but melting into his hands? "Why not?"

"Just don't."

She moved toward him, needing to be closer, wanting to merge with his shadow, to take on his pain and understand. "You're going to have to do better than that if you want me to understand."

Couldn't she see how hard this was for him? Couldn't she see what she was doing to him? "I'm not asking for your understanding, I'm asking for your cooperation."

"My cooperation?" She didn't understand. In the background, Humphrey Bogart was asking the piano player to play "As Time Goes By," the song that everyone remembered from *Casablanca*. Dottie hardly heard. "What kind of cooperation?"

There was just so much a man could successfully withstand. "You shouldn't smell this good, or look this good, or sit on my sofa without your shoes."

Dottie looked down at her bare toes and wiggled them before looking up into Shea's face. "Looks like I'm flunking cooperation."

"Looks like."

"Might as well flunk it all the way." Dottie put her arms around his neck.

"What about the movie?" Even as he asked, Shea placed his hands on her hips and moved Dottie onto his lap.

Without looking, Dottie pointed the remote control over her shoulder in the VCR's general direction and clicked it off. Her eyes never left his. She was afraid the intensity would disappear. "I've already seen it."

Her mouth was too close to avoid, her presence too overwhelming to ignore. Shea framed her face with his hands and brought his lips to hers.

The first touch ignited all the kegs of powder he thought so safely under lock and key. He wasn't safe, not with her. Not now, not ever. She represented danger, all the elements that thrilled him, that awakened his senses and made them keen. All the elements that Shea had thought he had left behind.

Her mouth tasted of fresh strawberries. It went beyond the lipstick she used, beyond anything tangible that he could have shrugged off. He had a craving and the craving could only be satisfied by her.

His lips skimmed the planes of her face, slowly, carefully, as if he was creating a picture of her in his mind to press in the pages of time.

She felt his hands as they moved along her body, touching, gentling, arousing. He made a torrent of emotions flood through her, engulfing each other until her head was spinning and her very breath was gone. She felt his body, hard and ready, from want of her.

He wanted her so badly that he ached from the deprivation. Yet he knew that this was not a woman he could walk away from once he had sampled all there was, once he had felt her body yield to his. He'd been trapped. And in danger of once more being responsible for someone else's welfare. Someone else's life.

Shea couldn't let himself go, much as he yearned to. "Dottie."

She saw the withdrawal in his eyes before he said anything. She moved away, rigidly holding herself in, refusing to tremble. With a hand that shook only slightly, she reached for the remote control and clicked the movie back on.

"That's one way to get through the credits," she murmured, slowly drawing a deep breath. It didn't help. Her pulse was still beating crazily.

"Dottie." He searched desperately for a way to make her understand without sharing his burden. "I—"

"Shh. You'll miss the dialogue." She didn't want to hear any excuses and she knew that he wasn't ready to tell her the truth.

Shea settled back to watch a movie he had heard about but had never seen. There was nothing he could really say to explain. There was no way to make someone else understand the burden he carried. The only one who understood was Louisa. And she held him as accountable for Sandra's death as he held himself.

It was the only thing they had ever agreed on, he thought with an ironic smile.

Without thinking, he reached out and took Dottie's hand, wrapping his fingers around it. Dottie smiled at him and went on watching.

At least it was something. One tiny step for Dottie McClellan, one giant step for progress, she thought.

Chapter Eleven

Dottie had never known six weeks to fly by so fast, even at the pace she normally kept. Her life was evolving at a brisk clip. Even her practice was beginning to take shape. In the last two weeks, she had acquired two patients. A seven-year-old boy, small for his age, who was too intelligent to blend in and had withdrawn almost completely from everyone around him. And a ten-year-old whose parents had suddenly discovered that he had an alcohol problem and had had one for the last two years.

That took away two hours a week physically and several more hours mentally. The rest of the time belonged to Al. And to Shea.

Dottie did what she could to answer all of Al's questions whether it was about art, music or just about being a woman. Her aim was, above all, to make Al feel like a complete, confident person. This included a shopping spree at the end of the six weeks to prepare her for Louisa's visit.

"It's hard to imagine that all she wanted to talk about at the beginning of the summer was baseball," Shea commented as he watched Al model the dress she and Dottie had bought that afternoon. There was no doubt about it, his little girl was a young lady now. He felt bittersweet pride running through him.

She had styled and curled Al's hair and applied just the barest hint of makeup. That and the dress expertly hid the tomboy within. Dottie sat on the hassock, admiring her handiwork. "A person has to broaden her horizons, right Al?"

"Right." Al twirled around one more time, clearly enjoying the way her skirt felt as it flared out and then wound itself around her legs.

Dottie rose from the hassock. Except for what was in the video room, she was beginning to doubt that Shea owned a comfortable piece of furniture. "The whole idea behind this," Dottie placed her arm around Al's shoulders, "is to remember that you can be both. There's no reason in the world why you can't play on the softball team and still know the difference between a waltz and a samba."

"You've taught her to dance, too?" He would have liked to have seen that.

"Why not?" Dottie asked. "I'm a potpourri of information."

That you are, he thought. *That and more.*

"So?" Al flounced before her father impatiently. "Do you like it?" She spread out her dress.

Shea pulled her onto his lap. Al draped an arm around his neck as she waited for his response. "I think it's beautiful. And so are you." He dropped a quick kiss on her cheek.

Al looked down at the creamy pink skirt. "Think Grandmother will like it?"

"Grandmother," Dottie put in, "will see beyond the dress and love the girl."

There was no mistaking the look on Shea's face. "Um, Al, why don't you go change?" she suggested. "I want to talk to your Dad for a minute."

"Sure thing." Al rose to her feet, smoothing out the dress carefully. She turned to her father. "Grandmother's coming tomorrow, right?"

"Right." The displeasure in Shea's voice was obvious. "She arrives tomorrow morning. I've invited her over for dinner tomorrow night."

Al nodded and ran off to change. Dottie could see the girl's nervous anticipation in the way she moved. This was going to be some visit, she thought.

Shea waited until Al had left the room. He looked at Dottie. "Will you come to dinner?"

She'd hoped that he'd ask. "Yes, on one condition."

Shea looked at Dottie in surprise. A condition? That didn't sound like her. "Which is?" he asked guardedly.

He was uncomfortable and he wanted her there for moral support. She hated doing this, but maybe she could use the situation to get him to open up. It was for his own good, their own good. "That you tell me what there is between you and your mother-in-law."

He turned away as he shrugged. "Just the usual kind of in-law thing."

"I don't think so."

This time, she wasn't going to back away. She was tired of him nursing a wound like an old bear. She could help him. She *wanted* to help him, wanted him to want her to help. This was part of loving. If he didn't open up then they could never have a truly good relationship.

Dottie moved around to face him. She saw the dark, warning look in his eyes. Taking a deep breath, she plunged in.

"Sometimes it helps to talk things out." She wasn't getting anywhere. She wanted to shake him. She settled for just holding onto his arms. "*Every time* it helps to talk things out."

For a moment, he wanted to shrug her off, but then he remained where he was, not breaking contact. She was forcing him to do something he couldn't do. He couldn't share. That would be weak. Instinctively he resisted. "I'm not a talker, Dottie. That's your department."

"Maybe you should learn," she coaxed, plumbing the depths of her patience when she wanted to scream at him, "instead of letting whatever it is eat at you." His face was impassive. Dottie sighed and dropped her hands to her sides.

Turning, she picked up her purse from the table and began to walk out of the room. "Tell Al we still have a date next Sunday at my place."

He stared at the back of her head a minute, uncomprehending. "Then you won't come tomorrow?"

Dottie swung around and he saw the frustration she felt shining in her eyes. "Not if you won't talk to me. Not if you won't trust me to listen. What's the point? I can't help what I don't understand." She lifted her head proudly, fighting back tears. "Goodbye, Shea."

She turned and walked out of the room, gambling. Hoping. Wondering if she had enough courage to make it to the front door before she swung around and beat on him with both fists.

Shea watched her go. And then something snapped inside. He couldn't let her leave. He had told himself that he didn't need her, that he didn't need anyone. That he would *never* need anyone because it was better, safer that way. But he had lied and now he knew it. He had loved that old man, and Flanders had died suddenly. He'd loved Sandra and she had died. He'd loved and needed. And felt both controlled and angered by his inability to let that go.

But there was no way around it.

"All right, damn it, have it your way."

Dottie stopped. *Thank you, God.*

She fought back the smile of relief that highlighted her whole being before she turned around. "It's not a matter of *my* way—"

He cut the distance between them in a few short strides, torn between wanting to sweep her into his arms and throttle her for making this happen to him again.

"Isn't it?" He looked down into her face, a face that he had come to know so well in such a short amount of time. "I wish she had been like you."

"Sandra?"

He nodded. "Yes."

Taking her hand, he drew Dottie back into the living room. Athena emerged from the kitchen, took one look in their direction, and retreated. This was not the time to intrude.

"Sandra was sweet and kind and giving. And her mother sucked her dry."

Dottie took on the role of a mediator naturally. "Sometimes parents expect a lot—"

Shea remembered the frustration Sandra went through. The pain. "Louisa expected too much. Perfection. Nothing Sandra ever did satisfied her." He dragged a hand through his hair. "Louisa always found fault with Sandra, beating her spirit into the ground."

And he had been drawn to the vulnerable woman who needed protecting, Dottie thought. Her heart softened, picturing him as a knight in shining armor. That was probably the way Sandra had thought of him, too.

"It got worse after I married her."

"You lived with Louisa?"

He laughed shortly, surprised at her question. "Hell, no. I would have lived in the street before I lived in that woman's house. Besides, there was no need. I had my own business by then. Nothing great, but it was enough to support us. And Al when she came along." He had had to cut corners, but it was different that time. There was someone struggling with him, someone to make it all mean something, to make it all worthwhile. "Sandra had some money she inherited from both of her grandmothers. She insisted I use it to build up my business."

Dottie had a feeling that his pride had made him resist in the beginning. That made what came after even worse. "And Louisa thought you were using Sandra."

"It was a classic case," Shea answered bitterly. "Louisa never stopped trying to force Sandra to leave me. She came over and started in on her again that night—"

Abruptly, he stopped. The memory was too painful to drag up again. He had replayed it too often in his own mind already.

"Yes?" Dottie wanted to plead with him to go on. He had to get this out of his system and out in the open. "What about that night?"

Part of surviving meant being self-sufficient, strong, being exceedingly tough. That led to being a loner, to an inability to share feelings. There was weakness in emotions. His emotions made him feel weak and it went against his grain to feel that way. But Dottie, with her simple way of caring, of giving, made him want to share despite all his common sense that told him not to.

"The night Sandra was killed, Louisa came here and there was a scene." He closed his eyes a moment, remembering. When he opened them again, he saw the sympathy in Dottie's eyes as she waited for him to continue. "Louisa had found out that Sandra had gone into her trust fund and taken money out for our store." His mouth twisted in a grim, icy smile. "She accused me of marrying Sandra for her money, that she knew no one would want such a spineless jellyfish if there weren't money involved." The anger he felt built as he repeated the words. "I ordered her out of my house, telling her to stay away from both of us."

"Instead Sandra fled, crying that she couldn't take being pulled in two directions any more." He stopped, his lips dry. Tears clawed at his throat. "It was raining that night. Hard. Sandra jumped into the car and drove away before I could stop her." His voice grew tight as he tried to distance himself, but failed. "I saw the car careen down the street and into an oncoming van." He let out a breath slowly. It didn't diminish the pain in his face. "She died instantly."

"Oh Shea, I'm so very sorry." Dottie put her arms around him. The tension was still there in his body. He wouldn't let himself be held or comforted. She refused to let go.

He looked down at Dottie. "Louisa blames me for Sandra's death." Gently disentangling himself, Shea walked to the window and looked out, seeing nothing. Not wanting to see anything. "And so do I."

Dottie was horrified. She came up behind him. "Why?"

Didn't she see? "If I hadn't made Sandra chose between us—"

She wasn't going to let him finish. The idea was ridiculous. "Sandra would have lived out her entire life, frustrated, unhappy, never managing to live up to her mother's expectations."

He swung around to face her. "But at least she would have been alive."

But Dottie shook her head. "Sometimes the quality of life is more important than the quantity." She placed her hands on his shoulders, searching his face for a sign that he understood what she was trying to tell him. "You made her happy. You gave her a child. You helped fulfill her. Seven years of happiness is worth a lifetime of emptiness in trade."

"Oh God, Dottie." Shea took her into his arms and held her for a long moment. "I wish I could believe that."

"There's no reason in the world not to." She moved back to look at him.

He released her. "Maybe."

She saw doubt lingering in his eyes. Perhaps she had planted the seed of change. Now she had to hope it would germinate and flourish.

"So what time do you want me?"

"Now." The word slipped out inadvertently, bringing surprise and then a slow smile with it as Shea looked at her.

Dottie laughed softly. "I meant for dinner."

Dinner. The ordeal yet to come. His smile faded. "Louisa gets here at six."

"I'll be here at four," she promised, threading her arms around his waist. They still had a little unfinished business to attend to. "To hold whoever's hand needs holding."

He held her tightly, burying his face in her hair, in her fragrance. She felt so good, small, yet so strong. As he held on to her he felt himself changing. He could feel again without that sense of weakness that had always followed in tandem. "That's a lot of holding." He brushed away a wisp of hair from her forehead.

"I'm the woman for the job."

Yes, he thought as he bent to kiss her, he was beginning to believe that she was.

* * *

Louisa Taylor Babcott was a woman of medium stature with an imperial manner about her that made her seem larger somehow. Her gray eyes were cold as she greeted Shea and briefly acknowledged his introduction to Dottie. But Dottie saw a flicker of warmth and something more in the woman's eyes when she looked at Al.

"You look like her," Louisa said, taking both of Al's hands in hers. "Except," she touched a strand and pursed her lips in disapproval, "your hair should be longer."

"She likes it short," Shea told Louisa, his voice brittle.

Al's hand flew to her hair. "But I'm letting it grow out," she volunteered quickly.

Louisa nodded slowly. "I'm sure it will look better that way."

It was happening again. Louisa was already trying to lay the groundwork for a schism. Shea bit back the angry bile that rose into his mouth as he remembered another time, another dinner. It wasn't going to happen here, not if he could stop it.

Dottie reached for Shea's hand and squeezed it. She could see the tension in his shoulders, feel it in the air. She wished there was something she could do to put a stop to it. For all their sakes. But for now, all she could do was watch the drama unfold.

Al, pleased at finally having a visible grandmother, chattered through dinner, wavering between excitement and nerves. Each time her enthusiasm caught fire, Louisa would comment politely that ladies did not get carried away and Al would retreat a little.

And each time it happened, Dottie had to bite back her words.

Louisa dominated the conversation. Dottie was certain that the woman knew of no other way to proceed. What surprised Dottie was that Shea said little during the course of the meal. It was, she thought, as if he didn't quite trust himself to speak other than to occasionally comment on something Al said.

The discomfort felt in the gathering was evident even in the way Athena served the meal.

"I'm surprised to see that you're still with them, Athena," Louisa commented as the other woman set down a silver coffee service on the dining table. "After all, you were with Sandra first. One would think that after she was gone—" Louisa's voice purposely drifted off, letting the woman fill in her own meaning.

Athena lifted her head proudly, looking, Dottie thought, every inch as regal as Louisa. There was no love lost between the two women. Athena's dark brown eyes grew sharp. "I am the housekeeper for the Delany family. Where would it be that I would want to go?"

Louisa looked annoyed that Athena would answer her in such a manner. "Some place more—fitting."

"There is no place more fitting. Sugar, Mrs. Babcott?" Athena pushed the sugar bowl closer to the woman's china cup before she turned and walked back into the kitchen like a victorious soldier.

Louisa slowly stirred in one teaspoon of sugar, her eyes on Athena's retreating back. "She hasn't lost her sharp tongue, I see."

The very sound of her critical voice grated on Shea's nerves. "Some things don't mellow with time," Shea said pointedly.

Crossed swords at forty paces, Dottie thought. So far, the evening hadn't been a success, although the participants had been relatively polite. She looked from Shea to Louisa, feeling as if she was sitting on a powder keg, waiting for it to explode.

Abandoning her coffee after taking only one sip, Louisa rose. "I'd like to adjourn to the living room if you don't mind." She tossed the words out to Shea as she left the room.

Dottie rose quickly. "Justifiable homicide is still illegal in this country," she whispered to Shea, hoping to coax a smile from him.

"A pity," he murmured. For Al's sake, he held on to his temper. It wasn't easy.

Louisa had positioned herself on the Louis XIV sofa and patted the cushion next to her as she looked at her grand-daughter.

The queen, holding court, Dottie thought.

When Al sat down, Louisa asked, "How would you like to come to Europe with me, Alessandra?"

Al's eyes grew wide. She thought of all the things she and Dottie had talked about over the last six weeks. "Europe?" she echoed. "Paris?"

Louisa smiled indulgently, triumph shining in her eyes now. "Yes, if you'd like. I could show you—"

Shea broke his promise to himself. "Al can't go. She's on a softball team."

The powder keg was about to blow. Dottie braced herself.

"Softball team?" Louisa spit out the words as if Shea had informed her that the girl had leprosy. She looked clearly offended that her granddaughter would even *think* of participating in such a thing.

"Yes." Shea turned to his daughter. "Al, why don't you go and get your scrapbook for your grandmother?"

Al bit her lower lip in distress as she looked from Louisa's angry face to her father's. "But I—"

"Get it," Shea ordered in a voice he had never used with her before. "Please." His eyes remained on Louisa's.

"Shea," Dottie began with a warning note.

"I know what I'm doing." Shea waved away Dottie's words. Reluctantly, Al left the room to retrieve her scrapbook.

"Do you? I seriously doubt that." Louisa was on her feet. "How could you allow her to play in a—a dirty sport like that?"

Shea crossed his arms before him, striking a nonchalant attitude. Dottie knew better. "Because she wanted to," he told his mother-in-law.

Louisa waved a hand at him in annoyance, dismissing his explanation. "Obviously, you haven't learned anything in six years." Her expression told them that she had expected as much. "Alessandra is a young lady who needs someone to show her the finer things in life, who'll mold her—"

He had had enough. "The way you molded Sandra?"

The gray eyes glinted. "Sandra was weak. She needed my help. I only wanted the best for her."

All the pain, all the old wounds were still fresh. "And you never felt she achieved it."

Louisa was outraged at being challenged this way. "How I raised my daughter was my business."

But she had met her match. "And how you tortured my wife was mine. You're not getting your hands on my daughter. You're not ruining her life, too."

Louisa laughed, as if his words had no meaning. Dottie longed to intervene. "If she wants to go to Europe with me, I'll take her."

"The hell you will. The decision is mine to make, not yours."

Louisa played her ace card. "As long as you are her guardian."

Dottie saw the rage wash over Shea's face. His hands were clenched into fists at his side. "I knew you'd do this." Repeating the words he had said six years ago, Shea said, "I'll thank you to leave my house."

Louisa couldn't resist one parting short. "A house bought with Sandra's money."

It hadn't been Sandra's money. It had been his. It was something he had insisted on, filled with a pride he hadn't known until then existed. But he didn't feel as if he had to explain any of that to Louisa. "That's all you've ever cared about, money and possessions."

Pain entered the woman's eyes. "I cared about my daughter."

He didn't believe her, not for a moment. "Then why didn't you ever let her know?"

She had had more than enough. She didn't have to stand for this. "You killed my daughter, I won't give you my granddaughter!"

With a cry filled with anguish, Louisa turned and left the room. Shea made no attempt to stop her. He turned away and stood by the window, trying to compose himself. Everything felt raw inside.

Dottie couldn't stand this. "Shea—"

"Leave it alone, Dottie," he snapped. Relenting, Shea turned to look at her. "I'm sorry. It's not your fault. It's mine. I shouldn't have had you here to see this."

"I'm glad you did. I understand things a lot better now." She placed her hand on his shoulder. "Don't worry. It's going to be all right."

He looked toward the empty doorway and heard the front door slam in the distance. "Damn right it is. She's not going to get her hands on Al."

Al walked into the room, her scrapbook in her hands. She had heard the raised voices. "What's going on? Where's Grandmother?"

He tried to smile at her and found that he couldn't. Louisa had taken a lot from him. "She had to leave suddenly."

Al stepped back, confused, angry. "You sent her away, didn't you?" She didn't understand. She only knew that there was something between her father and grandmother. Something that prevented a family unit from existing. She felt deprived. "Why? We were going to talk."

"No," Shea said quietly, trying to hold onto his anger. "She was going to talk and you were going to listen."

"I don't get it." She shook her head, blinking away tears. "Would that have been so bad?"

"In this case, yes."

Al threw the scrapbook on the floor and fled the room. "Al!"

"Let her go, Shea," Dottie said. She knew how he felt, but there were times to back off. "She needs to be alone for a while. You're not the only one in turmoil about all this."

"Damn her," Shea muttered. He shoved his hands into his pockets, balling them into fists again. "Damn her for coming back."

And there were times, Dottie decided, not to back off. Quietly, she slipped out of the room.

"You are leaving, too?" Athena asked just as Dottie reached the front door.

"With any luck, I'll be back."

Athena understood. "That will take a powerful lot of luck, lady."

Dottie smiled. "I've always been lucky."

Chapter Twelve

Dottie couldn't sit by idly while this situation evolved in the terrible direction it was heading. These were people she cared about and she wasn't going to watch them suffer. She *had* to do something to stop it. She knew that Shea would probably be angry with her for interfering, but she had no choice.

Taking a deep breath, she raised her hand and knocked on the door of hotel room number eight-twenty-five.

There was no answer. She was about to knock again when the door opened. Louisa, her eyes slightly reddened, looked at her in surprise. It had been a scant thirty minutes since angry words had passed in Shea's living room. Her voice was cold, belittling. "What are *you* doing here?"

"Helping, I hope." Dottie kept her tone friendly, but there was no mistaking the fact that Louisa was not about to intimidate her. "May I come in?"

Louisa looked as if she was about to refuse, but then she lifted her shoulders indifferently and let them drop. She gestured carelessly into the room as she stepped back. "Did he send you?"

Dottie smiled and shook her head. The woman didn't know him at all if she thought that Shea would send someone to take his part. He fought his own battles. "He doesn't even know I'm here. He'd probably be very angry if he knew." Dottie glanced around. It wasn't a room, it was a suite of rooms. It must be nice to be used to only the very best. Dottie thought of the three rooms, all unoccupied save for one woman. And probably very lonely as well.

Louisa looked at Dottie with a small amount of interest. "And that doesn't matter to you, that he's angry?"

Not waiting to be asked, Dottie sat down on the sofa. "I'd rather he wasn't, but that doesn't change what I have to do."

Louisa remained standing. It gave her the advantage of height. It evidently annoyed her that it didn't affect Dottie in the least. "Which is?"

Dottie patiently folded her hands in her lap. "To try to talk to you before a lot of people are hurt. Including you."

"Why should you care about my being hurt?" There was suspicion in every syllable. "You don't even know me."

No, but she knew loneliness when she saw it. "I think I know you better than you think I do."

The sincerity in Dottie's voice made Louisa soften her superior tone just a little. "Just who are you in the scheme of things?"

"A friend," Dottie answered simply. "But it really doesn't matter who I am. What matters is you. And Shea and Al."

Louisa, her eyes never leaving Dottie's face, sat down on the far end of the sofa. "Alessandra."

Dottie smiled. Stubbornness she could understand very well. "She prefers to be called Al."

"That's so common," Louisa said loftily.

"But it's her choice," Dottie pointed out gently. "Choices are important for people to make, for people to feel that they have the freedom to make. Even wrong ones. It builds character. It's what makes people strong."

Louisa drew herself up indignantly. "Young woman, I don't care to be preached at—"

If she was looking for an argument, Louisa had taken on the wrong person. She was here as a peacemaker, not an instigator. "I'm not preaching, I'm talking. I think we really need to sit down and talk. I just witnessed a scene tonight that involved three very unhappy people." Dottie reached over and placed her hand on the two clasped ones in Louisa's lap. "People who are all going to be losers unless something is done to change all that."

Louisa looked down accusingly at Dottie's hand, but made no attempt to pull her own away. "Why are you telling me all this?"

Dottie smiled. It was a beginning. "Because it has to start somewhere. And you have as much to lose in this matter as Shea. Maybe more. You'll be completely alone."

Louisa would not accept sympathy easily. She didn't understand it. "*If* I lose."

Dottie nodded. "And maybe if you win," she added.

Louisa pulled her hands away, annoyed. "What *are* you talking about?"

At least she wasn't throwing her out. Dottie took heart from that. "If you *had* managed to get Sandra away from

Shea, do you think Sandra would have been grateful to you for that, for breaking up a happy marriage?''

Louisa rose and placed her hands on the back of the sofa, leaning over until her face was almost level with Dottie's. Each word she uttered was underlined. "She didn't know what happiness was.''

Dottie was undaunted. "I think she did. It just wasn't your definition of happiness. Sandra was desperately trying to be her own person, but she kept wanting to please you.''

Louisa shot her a piercing look. "I resent you standing there, telling me about my daughter.''

"I'm sitting,'' Dottie corrected.

The wind dropped from her sails at the casual modification. "What?''

Louisa's expression told Dottie she had made her point. "How does it feel to be corrected?''

"I don't like it.''

"Exactly.''

Louisa frowned. "Why shouldn't my daughter have wanted to please me?''

"Because it destroyed her.''

The simple answer was more than Louisa could bear. "Shea destroyed her. He killed her!''

Dottie shook her head. "No, Sandra has to take responsibility for something here, don't you think? She caved in. She couldn't stand to hear the two of you arguing.'' Dottie rose and placed her hand on the woman's shoulder, compassion in the gesture. "Maybe the blame lies everywhere. But there's no use in digging up the past except to learn from it. Don't make the same mistake again.''

Louisa looked at the hand on her arm, the understanding in Dottie's eyes. All the years she had lived abroad, alone, suddenly weighed heavily on her. "I just wanted what was best."

And the woman honestly believed that, Dottie thought sadly. "No one is saying that you didn't. But it wasn't the best for them." Dottie took the woman's hand in hers and squeezed warmly. "Why don't you come back with me to Shea's house and maybe we can resolve this thing once and for all so that everyone can finally get on with their lives. Together."

Louisa pulled her hand away. There was a touch of panic beneath the regal composure. "No, I can't."

"Yes," Dottie said firmly, "you can. The only thing stopping you is you. Don't you see what harm is being done? Do you want Al in the same position as Sandra was in? Torn between two people she loves? She's not a doll to be pulled back and forth in a self-serving tug-of-war. She's a young girl who needs a father *and* her grandmother."

The silence stretched out over several minutes. "All right," Louisa said quietly. "I'll come."

It was all coming to a head, just as he had always feared it would. Everything in his life that he had fought for. Nothing had ever come easily. If he had to fight for Al, he would. He wasn't about to turn and run. He knew things could get ugly. If Louisa wanted a custody fight, her battery of lawyers would try to drag his name through the mud. And he had supplied them with ammunition. There was a lot in his past he was ashamed of, a lot that Al didn't know about. It didn't negate the fact that he had overcome all this and had lived a spotless life ever since he had met Sandra.

He'd call his lawyer the first thing in the morning, he decided. It wouldn't hurt to be prepared.

Shea was on his way upstairs to try to talk to Al again when the doorbell rang. It caught Shea by surprise. It was after ten. Who would be calling at this hour?

"I'll get it, Athena," he called out. He was still having trouble controlling his newly aroused anger. Al was upstairs, crying, refusing to talk to him. Dottie had left without saying a word. And Louisa was threatening to rip his life apart. He was not in the best of moods to talk to any visitors.

He pulled the door open and then stared, speechless. Dottie was standing on his doorstep, next to Louisa.

Dottie's smile was tinged with both determination and uncertainty. She hoped that Shea would control his anger long enough for this to work. "Louisa would like to talk to you, Shea."

Louisa had never had anyone speak for her. Stunned, Shea could only nod as he stepped back. "All right." His voice was drained of emotion. "We'll talk in the living room."

Louisa proceeded ahead of him. Shea took the opportunity to pull Dottie over to the side. "What's this all about?" he whispered, both annoyed and confused. The next time he had expected to see Louisa was across a table with an army of lawyers between them. He certainly didn't feel like welcoming the woman into his house. Neither did he feel like talking to her at this late hour. She had caused enough trouble in his life for one evening.

"A peace treaty." Dottie tugged on his arm, urging him forward. "Now stop frowning," she whispered back, "you'll get wrinkles."

The woman was exasperating, he thought. Crazy. He couldn't begin to understand the way her mind worked. Shea saw absolutely no reason for Dottie to have brought

Louisa back. Louisa had made herself perfectly clear. She wanted to do to Al just what she had done to Sandra. He would die before he let that happen.

Dottie looked at Shea's face as they entered the room and knew this wasn't going to be easy. What she had on her hands were two mountains and no Mohammad. It was going to take an earthquake to get them together.

If necessary, she was ready to do some shaking.

"Shea, Louisa, please sit." Dottie gestured toward the sofa. Shea looked at her in surprise. "Sit," she repeated firmly. "You're both taller than I am and I'd like to have the advantage for a moment." She waited until Shea sat down.

"This is ridiculous," Shea said.

"Humor me." She looked from one to the other. "I think we're agreed that you both loved Sandra and that you both love Al."

No, they weren't in agreement on that. "She never loved Sandra," Shea interjected.

"Yes, I did," Louisa insisted angrily. "I loved her very, very much."

He refused to listen to lies. "Then why didn't you ever show her?"

"I did." Louisa looked at him haughtily. "She had everything a girl could ask for."

"Except a mother who showed her that she cared," Dottie pointed out.

They both looked at Dottie in surprise. "I didn't bring you two together for another shouting match. I want you to resolve this. You did and do both care. That is a given. Work from there."

Before I bash both your stubborn heads in.

Louisa lifted her chin and Dottie realized that it was to keep it from trembling. There were tears shining in the older woman's eyes.

"I don't know how to show affection." The unexpected confession agitated her. Louisa rose, clutching her purse tightly with both hands. "Don't you think I haven't gone over that night in my mind a hundred times?" Louisa cried as she turned to Shea. "A thousand times? Wondering, perhaps, if it was I who sent her running off into the night? If it was I who was responsible for her death? Don't you think I'd do anything to have her back? She was my *daughter*." Louisa held back a sob. "My only child."

Shea wanted to keep his anger fresh, to hold it to him like a shield. But he couldn't, not in the face of Louisa's anguish. "Then why are you trying to do the same thing with Al?"

Louisa turned away. With her hands on her shoulders, Dottie gently made her face Shea. Louisa picked at her purse strap. "I don't know any other way. You'll keep her from me if I don't." She looked away again, ashamed of admitting her emotions. "And I don't want to spend the autumn of my years alone and lonely." Her voice grew bitter. "An old woman people pity because no one cares."

He didn't want to feel sorry for her. But he did. He couldn't help it. Dottie had showed him the way and now he couldn't go back.

So much time had been lost because of pride, Shea thought. "I would have never denied you Al's company. You didn't have to resort to luring her away to Europe. You're her grandmother, for God's sake. And blood, as you always kept telling Sandra, is important." He spread his hands out, clearing the air. "If you want Al to be part of your life, move back to the States permanently. You can see her any time you like.''

Louisa was very quiet as she took in the scope of his words. She sank down on the sofa again, numbed. ''It seems I've misjudged you, Shea,'' she said finally, pulling all the dignity together she could muster. ''I've had my lawyers investigate you thoroughly. You need neither my money nor my goodwill.''

So she had been planning a custody battle even before she had arrived. ''All I need is a grandmother for Al.''

''And that you shall have.'' Awkwardly, Louisa offered him her hand. ''I'm sorry. Can you find it in your heart to forgive me?''

He knew that wasn't easy for her. He doubted that she had ever asked anyone's forgiveness before and had never dreamed of asking it of him. He wanted to blame her, to make her suffer the way he had all these years. But there was nothing to be gained by it. Seeking revenge for the past was fruitless. There was the future to think of. And Al.

Besides, he could see that she had already suffered enough. They all had.

Shea took her hand. ''I learned a long time ago that revenge is a very bitter meal to digest.''

Louisa blinked back tears as she held onto his hand. Apologizing didn't rest well with her. She took a deep breath. ''I can move back. There's nothing to hold me back there and everything, it appears, to hold me here.'' She rose again. ''Now, if you'll be so kind as to call me a taxi, Shea,'' she smiled, ''I'll get back to my hotel room and start making plans for the rest of my life.''

''I can take you back,'' Dottie offered. ''After all, I brought you here.''

"Yes, you did. And I shall be eternally grateful for that." She took Dottie's hand in hers and held it for a moment. The gesture spoke volumes. "But you stay here. I've imposed on you enough for one day."

Shea looked at Dottie over the woman's head. Was this really Louisa? Dottie, just by being herself, by refusing to give up, had worked magic in the space of half an hour, undoing six years of grief and fifteen years of bad blood. The woman was incredible.

"I guess I'd better be going, too," Dottie said after Louisa had departed in the taxi Shea had called. "It's getting late."

He glanced at his watch. He didn't want her going anywhere. Ever again. "Funny, I feel like the evening is just beginning."

He had lost her. Maybe the stress of the evening had confused him. She looked around for her purse. God, it had been a long day. "Do you want me to come by tomorrow?"

"Sure." He looked at her suspiciously. "Why wouldn't I?"

Dottie shrugged, suddenly feeling a little uneasy. What if it was over? What if she had inadvertently brought about the end of her usefulness? Louisa and Shea were reconciled. A family unit was formed. Everything was perfect.

What if he didn't need her anymore? What if she was now just a fifth wheel? All she had to go on as to how he felt about her was her own interpretation of things. Maybe she was wrong.

"Well," she began slowly, pretending to be preoccupied with looking for her purse. "Al's 'transformation' is well on its way and now with Louisa planning to stay on, she can take over the task of smoothing out the rough edges—"

"And who," he asked, taking her hand, "is going to take over the task of warming my heart, of making my days and nights worth living?"

For once in her life, Dottie was afraid to leap to a conclusion, even though it seemed to be written out for her on a giant cue card. "I didn't think you felt as if you needed anyone."

"I didn't." He saw her face fall. How adorable she was, he thought. And how damn lucky he was. "I didn't *think* I needed anyone. You showed me differently. You showed me I was an idiot for feeling like that."

Dimples appeared in the corners of her mouth. "Not exactly an idiot—"

"Yes, exactly an idiot," he contradicted. "I'd opened up a little with Sandra, but after she died, I went back to my old ways. I always felt that dependence of any kind was a weakness. The weak don't survive. I was a survivor and I had Al to survive for. It made my resolve that much firmer, my shell that much harder." He smiled. "But you managed to crack it anyway."

Her eyes fluttered shut as he kissed each cheek, then lightly brushed his lips against hers. "You made me want you. You made me love you and now you're going to have to take the responsibility for your rash actions."

She squirmed a little against him, enjoying the feel the rush of his desire created. "Nothing rash about what I did," she grinned.

His expression grew serious. "Then you're not sorry?"

"Sorry? Shea Delany, I'm only sorry that you were so slow to come around."

He played with the ends of her hair. "I had my reasons."

"You had ghosts," she corrected. "We all have ghosts of one form or another. But they can't hurt us if we don't let them. And there's so much to life if we just reach out and take it."

He pulled her even closer against him. "I'm reaching."

She smiled up into his face. "You never had to reach far."

He shook his head. "Farther than you'll ever understand." He dug into his pocket and handed her a small box. "Here, I've been carrying this around for five weeks. I believe it's yours."

Intrigued, Dottie opened the box and then sucked in her breath. "It's the cameo brooch."

"Not exactly your run-of-the-mill engagement ring," he admitted, "but then, you're not exactly your run-of-the-mill fiancée, either."

"Fiancée?"

"You know," he kissed her neck and heard her moan, "the term that comes before wife."

Dottie swallowed. "Wife?"

He looked around. "Is there an echo in here?"

She laughed, delighted. "Must be, because I don't think I'm hearing right."

"Yes, you are." He kissed each corner of her mouth, tilting the room as he did so. "Marry me, Dottie?"

She stared down at the brooch. It was impossibly beautiful. And she was impossibly in love. "Are you sure? Are you very, very sure?" She searched his face for signs of hesitation. And found none.

He grazed each eyelid lightly with his lips, sending her pulses scrambling. "Sure that I'll go crazy if you don't. You've shown me the light, Dottie." He gathered her against him. "Don't take it away. Don't leave me in the dark again."

Her fingers closed over the brooch. "Not a chance, fella. It's got a shelf life of a thousand years."

"I'll hold you to that." His mouth closed over hers.

Epilogue

"She's giving us tickets?" Dottie stared at the two airplane tickets in Shea's hands. It had only been a little more than forty-eight hours since the reconciliation. This seemed like a very impressive peace offering. But then, as Athena had commented earlier that day, there was nothing small about Louisa.

"Two round-trip tickets to Italy." He placed them in her hand for examination. "She has a villa in Italy. She wants us to stay there for the honeymoon."

"I insist on it," Louisa added as she entered the living room.

Al fairly bounced in after her. The girl's happiness was unmistakable. Finally, after wanting one for so long, she was going to have a real family, a grandmother, two actually, she amended, thinking of Mama Marino, an aunt, uncles, a cousin and another one soon.

And a mother.

She beamed at Dottie. It had all started with her. Impulsively, she gave Dottie a hug.

Surprised, Dottie hugged back. But she looked at the tickets uncertainly. "I don't know. Al—" She didn't know if she liked the idea of leaving Al so soon after bringing about all these changes in the young girl's life.

"Will be fine," Louisa assured her. "I'm going to stay here and we're going to get reacquainted. After all, six years is a very long time." She closed Dottie's hand over the tickets. "Now you take those and enjoy yourself. And thank you," Louisa added in a whisper before she turned away.

"Grandmother." Al followed Louisa out. "How do you feel about baseball games?"

Louisa paused in the doorway, considering the question. Dottie listened with interest as she and Shea exchanged looks.

"I don't know," Louisa admitted honestly. "But one is never too old to learn something new." She winked at Dottie, and then placed her arm around Al's shoulder, leaving the room.

"I guess we've run out of excuses," Dottie said philosophically.

"I guess so." Shea nodded, matching her mood.

"We'll just have to go through with the wedding." Dottie turned the tickets over in her hand.

"Looks that way," he agreed.

"It'll make everyone happy." Her solemn expression could only survive for so long. A grin broke through. "I always believe in making everyone happy."

"Very magnanimous of you." Shea thought of Al and of Mama Marino. "Know what'll make them even happier?"

"What?"

"If we come home from Italy pregnant." He was looking forward to accomplishing that little labor of love. They might not even leave the villa the entire time they were in Italy. He wouldn't mind.

"We?" She raised one eyebrow, trying hard not to laugh. "You're planning on getting pregnant with me?"

He pulled her into his arms. The tickets flew out of her hand and fell on the floor. "I plan on doing everything with you for the rest of my life."

This time she did laugh. The room rang with her joy. She put her arms around his neck. God, but she loved him. "Then it should be a very interesting life."

"My sentiments," Shea said against her mouth just before he kissed her, "exactly."

* * * * *

® *Silhouette Romance*®

LONG, TALL TEXANS

DONAVAN
Diana Palmer

Diana Palmer's bestselling LONG, TALL TEXANS series continues with DONAVAN....

From the moment elegant Fay York walked into the bar on the wrong side of town, rugged Texan Donavan Langley knew she was trouble. But the lovely young innocent awoke a tenderness in him that he'd never known...and a desire to make her a proposal she couldn't refuse....

Don't miss DONAVAN by Diana Palmer, the ninth book in her LONG, TALL TEXANS series. Coming in January...only from Silhouette Romance.

LTT192

Silhouette Special Edition salutes

MOMENTS OF GLORY

from Lindsay McKenna

In a country torn with conflict, in a time of bitter passions, these brave men and women wage a war against all odds... and a timeless battle for honor, for fleeting moments of glory, for the promise of enduring love.

February: RIDE THE TIGER (#721) Survivor Dany Villard is wise to the love-'em-and-leave-'em ways of war, but wounded hero Gib Ramsey swears she's captured his heart... forever.

March: ONE MAN'S WAR (#727) The war raging inside brash and bold Captain Pete Mallory threatens to destroy him, until Tess Ramsey's tender love guides him toward peace.

April: OFF LIMITS (#733) Soft-spoken Marine Jim McKenzie saved Alexandra Vance's life in Vietnam; now he needs her love to save his honor....

SEMG-1

Take 4 bestselling love stories FREE

Plus get a FREE surprise gift!

Special Limited-time Offer

Mail to Silhouette Reader Service™

In the U.S.
3010 Walden Avenue
P.O. Box 1867
Buffalo, N.Y. 14269-1867

In Canada
P.O. Box 609
Fort Erie, Ontario
L2A 5X3

YES! Please send me 4 free Silhouette Romance® novels and my free surprise gift. Then send me 6 brand-new novels every month, which I will receive months before they appear in bookstores. Bill me at the low price of $2.25* each—a savings of 34¢ apiece off cover prices. There are no shipping, handling or other hidden costs. I understand that accepting the books and gift places me under no obligation ever to buy any books. I can always return a shipment and cancel at any time. Even if I never buy another book from Silhouette, the 4 free books and the surprise gift are mine to keep forever.

*Offer slightly different in Canada—$2.25 per book plus 69¢ per shipment for delivery. Canadian residents add applicable federal and provincial sales tax. Sales tax applicable in N.Y.

215 BPA ADL9   315 BPA ADMN

Name	(PLEASE PRINT)

Address	Apt. No.

City	State/Prov.	Zip/Postal Code

This offer is limited to one order per household and not valid to present Silhouette Romance® subscribers. Terms and prices are subject to change.

SROM-91   © 1990 Harlequin Enterprises Limited

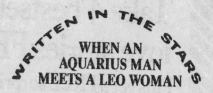

WRITTEN IN THE STARS

WHEN AN AQUARIUS MAN MEETS A LEO WOMAN

Unpredictable Aquarian Alex Sinclair liked his life as it was. He had his horses, his work and his freedom. So how come he couldn't—wouldn't—leave fiery veterinarian Katrina Rancanelli alone? The love-shy widow obviously wanted no part of him, but Alex was determined to hear her purr.... Lydia Lee's THE KAT'S MEOW is coming from Silhouette Romance this February—it's WRITTEN IN THE STARS.